For RooRoo,

In the words of The Beach Boys: -

"God only knows what I'd be without you."

Brian Wilson,
Tony Asher. 1966

BLOOD ACROSS THE POND

Nathan Weiss and Lionel Streat,
the heroes of

KILL OR CURE
AND

EL LION, A LIFE NOT LIVED

join forces on the trail of a vicious killer.

This is a work of fiction. To benefit the storyline, events are imagined and consequently historically inaccurate. Some of the place names are also fictional. Similarities between the names of any of the characters and persons living or deceased at the time of writing are entirely coincidental.

Editors: Ruth Lesser, Ikecaj Mulhans, Dean Lesser, Rocki Ezekiel

Cover Design: Shaina Lesser

12.00 Saturday 1st August 1914.
Prenk, a small town on the German-Russian Border.

Under a pale blue sky with scattered fluffy milk white clouds which were being chased across the heavens by the easterly wind, Abram and Lilya Weiss waited anxiously with their daughter Alexandria on the platform of the newly constructed railway station. A slight chill blew from the nearby Chenko River. They each clung onto one of Alexandria's hands. Abram savoured the final moments of physical contact with his beloved little princess. At twelve-years-old, she was the youngest of their five children, their only daughter and the light of his life. She was about to board the Trans-Siberian Railway with her mother and be taken away to safety. Abram bravely held back the tears as he considered the awful probability that he would never see his daughter again. He vainly tried to console himself in the knowledge that she would be escaping the atrocities which would otherwise undoubtedly threaten her life if she stayed. Eighteen years ago, he had moved from Berlin to settle in Russia with Lilya on her family's farm and start a family of their own. But in retaliation for Russia mobilizing its troops, his native Germans had declared that the two countries were at war. They would soon be on the march and sweeping all before them.

Lilya was taking Alexandria on the grueling five-day journey to England, where she would reluctantly place her in the care of her sister Natalia. She would then return to Russia alone. Natalia, who was two years older than Lilya, had fallen in love with an Englishman, David Simons, who ran a fur wholesale business in London and had journeyed to Russia to purchase pelts. Natalia worked in one of the nearby factories he had called upon. The attraction was instantaneous and mutual, and she left Russia with him to marry him in London in 1910.

Abram was equally concerned for the safety of his older children, but they were all strong teenage boys, and he needed their help with the work on the large family farm. Cows had to be milked and their sheds needed mucking out. Fields had to be ploughed and crops had to be sewn and reaped. Chickens had to be tended and their eggs collected. The working day was long, the farm chores were never ending, and Abram realised that he was not getting any younger. If he and his sons made it through the war unscathed, they would hopefully still have a successfully working farm at the end of it.

A distant whistle signalled the imminent arrival of the train. As it slowed to a halt at the platform, the guard waited for passengers to disembark and then called out for those who had been waiting to travel out to board.

Lilya, realising that the moment she had been dreading was almost upon her started to panic.

'Are you sure we are doing the right thing Abram?' she asked, grabbing his arm, the tears glistening in her eyes.

'Yes my darling, I am. The Germans will soon be upon us. At least this way Alexandria will be safe. Please, don't let her see you crying. She is frightened enough already.'

Abram knelt and hugged Alexandria so hard that she couldn't breathe. He stood up and turned around so that she couldn't see that despite himself tears were now streaming down his cheeks. But it didn't escape Lilya's notice. She smiled sympathetically and dabbed at his face with a handkerchief. He threw his arms up in despair and the three of them clung onto each other for the briefest of moments. The guard blew a shrill blast on his whistle and bellowed again for the last stragglers to board. Lilya clutched Alexandria's hand and pulled her away. They dejectedly clambered onto the train, entered a carriage and immediately found a window to peer out of. As the train pulled away, mother and daughter waved sadly at a distraught Abram until they could no longer see him.

Five days later, at Liverpool Street Station a similar scene took place when Lilya entrusted the care of her only daughter to Natalia. Only this time she was the one saying her goodbyes and boarding the train alone for the sad and long and lone journey home. More hugs were given, more tears were shed, and more distressed waves goodbye from Lilya at the train window as Alexandria and Natalia disappeared into the distance. Once the train was out of sight Natalia took Alexandria back to her home in Bethnal Green.

Germany invaded Russia on the first of September, the day after Lilya began her journey. Another five days after leaving Alexandria in London, Lilya's train pulled back into Prenk. The German troops who had been boarding every train which arrived and questioning the passengers, hauled Lilya onto the platform to interrogate her. Fighting for her life, she managed to wriggle free and attempted to flee. She didn't make twenty yards before she was mowed down in a hail of gunfire. She died instantly, unaware that three days before, her entire family had been murdered, the stock slaughtered and the farm burnt to the ground.

In London Alexandria thrived. She learned English quickly, did well in school and at sixteen she took a job in the local library on Bethnal Green Road. Her foster father, David Simons, was only ten years older than her, and she looked upon him more like one of the big brothers she had left behind in Russia.

Tragically he was killed in 1916 in the trenches in northern France and Alexandria was left alone with a grief-stricken Natalia.

11.00 Tuesday 6th July 1920. London.

Isaac Streat walked into the Bethnal Green library.

'Can I help you sir?' asked Alexandria.

'Yes please, I've been searching for a book on Regency furniture but I can't find anything.'

'OK sir, well let me see what I can do.'

Isaac was tall and solidly built, with a full head of sandy coloured hair. He was a carpenter who made reproduction furniture and he needed some pictures to work from. To his amazement Alexandria returned in just a few minutes holding a volume containing exactly what he was looking for.

'That's amazing, thank you,' he said.

He gazed at Alexandria. She had blossomed into a beautiful young woman with flaxen hair, striking emerald green eyes and an olive complexion. He tentatively began a conversation, which led to a lunchtime spent together the following day in the local café. He told her that he had returned from the war two years previously and served an apprenticeship in his uncle's factory. He had left there only weeks ago, taken on a small workshop and branched out on his own. Then his curiosity about Alexandria's accent got the better of him and he asked her to tell him about herself. He was an attentive listener. He sympathised and commiserated with her when with tear-filled eyes she softly and sadly spoke of her family's annihilation and the loss of David Simons.

'I'm really sorry,' Isaac said, hypnotized by her shining green eyes. 'You must have an amazing inner strength to have taken such awful blows and come through them like you have. To settle in a strange country as well.'

'Thank you Isaac,' she replied. 'You are very kind. But what choice did you and I have? It must have been dreadful for you as well. To fight in that terrible war, with your comrades dying all around you. We have to thank heaven that we have at least survived to make the best of what's left for us.'

Isaac was totally smitten. After that first lunch together they met regularly. Within six months he proposed. Alexandria readily accepted and they married in the March of 1921. In September 1922 Alexandria gave birth to their daughter Leila. Their son Solomon followed in

1924. Isaac's furniture business prospered and the family lived comfortably in a flat above his shop on the Mile End Road, just around the corner from Natalia.

4pm Wednesday 2nd September 1970. Edgewater.

Alone in her house, Sara answered the telephone.

'Hello,' she said. She no longer gave the telephone number when she answered. Since her son Lionel's stratospheric rise to fame as an England International World Cup winning footballer, which had been preceded by him winning a Gold medal in the 1500 meters at the 1968 Olympics, he'd advised her against doing so. She couldn't understand why.

'For heaven's sake,' she'd laughed. 'if someone has dialed the flipping number, then they've got it already haven't they?' But she erred on the side of caution and followed his advice.

'I'm calling from the office of The Prime Minister,' said the clipped voice of the man on the other end of the phone. 'May I speak with Mister Lionel Streat please.'

Assuming it was Eugene, her daughter Miriam's fiancé playing another one of his soppy pranks on her, Sarah laughed and said, 'Yes Eugene, and I'm Diana Dors!'

The person calling was used to people thinking that he was not who he said he was. So, he politely, and with a smattering of good humour himself said, 'Madam, I can assure you that I am Basil Armstrong, our Prime Mister Gavin Williams's personal secretary. I'm afraid that I don't know anyone called Eugene, and I'm also extremely sorry to have to tell you that you don't sound in the very slightest like Diana Dors! The Prime Minister has instructed me to call to invite your son to a reception at 10 Downing Street'.

The lengthy response took Sarah completely by surprise.

'Well', I'm, I'm' she stammered, 'I'm afraid my son isn't here. He hasn't lived with me for some time now.'

Lionel was still living with Johnny Graves's at his Rosemount Rovers club's digs. The two men got on like a house on fire, both on and off the field. Johnny really believed that the emergence of Lionel and the burgeoning success of their attacking partnership had played a major part in the resurrection of his own career.

'I know that Mrs Streat, he's not at the Rosemount training ground. I've tried there. They've finished training for the day and he's not answering the telephone at his home either. I was rather hoping that he would be with you. Might I leave a message with you please, in case you speak to him?'

'Of course,' Sarah said, 'I'm sure I'll speak to him later. He calls me most evenings.'

Armstrong gave her the telephone number, thanked her and said goodbye.

At six o'clock Lionel telephoned and Sarah excitedly told him about the earlier telephone call.

'Yes, I know.' Lionel said. 'Armstrong has left messages all over the place for me.'

'What's the reception for?' Sarah asked.

'They want to present me with some sort of award for what happened in Berlin. Apparently, the Germans do as well. Their Ambassador has been invited. That's only if I accept the invitation of course. It's for this Sunday afternoon.'

At the World Cup final in Berlin, a group of terrorists had kidnapped the Prime Minister's wife, Edith Williams. Lionel, who during the match had scored the winning goal, had subdued two of them and rescued her. He then overpowered the third who was waiting in the getaway car in the car park. His celebrity at home and in Germany went through the roof, to the point where the Germans had reluctantly almost forgiven him for beating them in the final.

'Why on earth wouldn't you?' Sarah asked, unable to disguise her astonishment.

'It's difficult mum. I can't really explain. I suppose I don't really want to be in the limelight.'

Sarah chuckled. 'Son, in case you haven't realised it, you've been in the limelight for over two years now. You should have got used to it. I've had to. I can't even go down the road to buy a quarter of smoked salmon without people coming up to me.'

'I know mum, and I'm sorry about that. But this is different. Anybody would have or should have done what I did in Germany. It's not something to be making a song and dance about. And it's not the same thing as being a footballer either. That's a job which I'm paid to do, and if I don't do it well, then I lose my place in the team, and quite rightly so.'

Sarah could sense in Lionel's voice that something was troubling him. Recently widowed, Sarah doted on both of her children. Miriam, Lionel's older sister had moved out only last month to live with Eugene, who was Lionel's manager in everything other than title. He advised Lionel on everything; advice which Lionel welcomed, along with Eugene's cheerful disposition and sense of humour, which was worse than disgusting. Now finding herself alone in the house, Sarah looked forward to Lionel's telephone calls. Since her husband had passed away Lionel had resumed joining her with Miriam and Eugene for Friday night dinner almost every week; except when he travelled overnight to away matches. Friday nights had become the highlight of Sarah's week. But now Lionel's tone was causing her some concern.

'What's troubling you Lionel? Is everything OK with you and Rebecca?'

'Of course it is. It's not that mum. I can't tell you anything, other than I'm thinking of packing football in.'

'But why? You're doing so well. Your name is on everybody's lips. I'll bet you that there isn't a conversation about football anywhere in the country, probably in the world, where your name doesn't come up. Have you discussed this with Eugene?'

'Yes, and funnily enough I think he agrees.'

'Well he and Miriam haven't said anything to me.'

'He won't mum. I asked him not to, at least not until everything has been settled. And anyway Miriam doesn't know yet. For that matter, neither does Rebecca.'

'And when will everything be settled?'

'After I've met with the Prime Minister,' Lionel said cryptically. He said it so casually it was as if meeting the Prime Minister was an every-day occurrence for him.

Sarah was silent while she considered what Lionel had just said. She thought back to the events outside the Berlin stadium in June, after the World Cup final, when Lionel had virtually single handedly apprehended the three terrorists. She remembered a remark that the Prime Minister had made, and suddenly it made sense to her. She instantly realised what was happening, and what was in Lionel's mind.

'OK,' she said quietly. 'Let me know what you decide. And Lionel?'

'Yes mum.'

'Please promise me you'll be careful.'

'Of course I will mum, of course.'

'See you Friday?' she asked.

'Sure, see you Friday. I'll tell you everything then, I promise. Can I invite Rebecca?'

'Of course you can. I love you son.'

'Thanks, I love you too mum. Oh, by the way.'

'Yes.'

'Keep Sunday afternoon clear.'

'I've already checked. It's clear, and even if it wasn't I'd cancel everything.'

Lionel laughed and hung up. What he was resisting telling his mother, mainly because he didn't want to worry her, was that since June he had already met with the head of the Prime Minister's protection team on a few occasions. His name was Harold Jonas. They had met at various locations and each time they had talked for an hour or more. Jonas was a bulldog of a man, who stood at just under six foot tall. He had a barrel chest and his greying hair was styled in a spiky crew cut. He had wild bushy eyebrows and a thin grey moustache which hovered menacingly above his upper lip. Despite Lionel's age, and not because of the incessant pressure that the Prime Minister, Gavin Williams, was putting him under, Jonas was keen to recruit Lionel, and had broached the subject every time they had spoken. When the PM's protection team leader, who answered to Jonas, returned from Germany, he'd supplied him with a full report detailing how Lionel had first rescued Edith Williams, the Prime Minister's wife, from the two terrorists who had captured her in the basement of the stadium. Without any regard to his personal safety he then volunteered to apprehend the third member of the group who was waiting in the getaway vehicle in the car park. Lionel casually walked outside, successfully overpowered the guy and handed him over to the German authorities, immediately becoming a hero in the German press. Lionel's capabilities were not like anything Jonas had seen or heard of before. Feeling certain that he'd be able to put them to good use, he had been very persistent in his pursuit of him.

Lionel admired Jonas's sincerity. His unequivocal love of his country was contagious, and every time they had met, he found that he was more drawn to the older man. Their last meeting had been that evening and Lionel had called Sarah as soon as it finished. Lionel told Johnny Graves, who usually drove him back to the house they shared after training, that he was going for a drink with an uncle. He didn't like lying to Johnny, but he couldn't possibly tell him what was going on. He hoped that he would understand. The last thing Lionel wanted to do was disappoint the iconic footballer who he had idolised for as long as he could remember.

Jonas picked him up and they went to the Thatched Barn on the A1. Over coffee Jonas asked Lionel again to consider working for him and to his delight Lionel agreed, but added that for now it would have to be a provisional agreement. When Jonas raised his eyebrows questioningly, Lionel explained that the problem he would have to overcome before he could definitely commit himself was his contract with Rosemount.

'Don't be concerned,' Jonas said, 'that's only a trivial issue, I'll deal with your manager.'

'You're not going to bump off Billy McPherson are you?' Lionel asked with a straight face.

'No of course not,' Jonas replied, then seeing a smile appear on Lionel's face he allowed himself a sardonic grin and said 'We'll just explain to the powers that be at your club that it would be advisable for them to release you to our service. I'm sure an adequate compensation package can be worked out, as of course can also a very satisfactory contract with yourself.'

'How will we explain my sudden disappearance from the team?'

'That's easy enough Lion. Oh, may I call you Lion, for the time being at least? Once you join the department I'm afraid it will have to be Streat. Rather like being back at school.

'No problem sir,' said Lionel. *"Not exactly like school,"* he thought. *"at least they won't be calling me weed."*

'Good, thank you. Anyway, we'll ask Rosemount to put out a press release saying that you picked up a career ending injury towards the end of your match on Saturday. Ligament damage or something like that.'

"I suppose I'm going to have to get used to these deceptions," thought Lionel, as Jonas paid the bill.

They walked out of the coffee lounge and back to Jonas's car. On the drive back to his digs Lionel wondered how Eugene would feel when he found out about him having his first business meeting without his mentor being present.

'What can I tell my family?' he asked Jonas. 'And anybody else who asks what I'm doing?'

'You can tell them that you've joined the Civil Service. You're working for the Home Office. You can't say any more than that I'm afraid. It's not a lie. That's where I work too and you'll be answering directly to me. It will all happen very quickly. We've already done our background checks. We know everything about you that we need to.'

'Really?' said Lionel.

'Yes really. You don't think I'd be talking to you otherwise do you?'

'I suppose not,' Lionel said.

Jonas pulled up outside Johnny's house.

'We'll be in touch with the club first thing on Monday, so this weekend will be your last match. Instead of going to training you'll be reporting to me at Whitehall. Are you OK with that?'

Lionel wasn't expecting things to move quite so quickly, but he nodded his agreement and they both smiled and shook hands. As he was getting out of the car Jonas said, 'You need to be sure about this Lion. Once you start there is absolutely no going back.'

'I'm sure.'

'Good. So, I'll see you on Sunday at Downing Street then. Goodnight…. Streat.'

Before Lionel could respond Jonas drove away.

Lionel had to keep his secret for three days and play at the weekend knowing it would be his last match. He was determined to make sure it would be a good one.

12.00 Wednesday 2nd September 1970. Rosemount Rovers.

Lionel called Armstrong during his lunch break to tell him that he would be attending on Sunday. It wasn't news for Armstrong. Jonas had already briefed him.

Lionel arranged to be collected from his mother's house at two o'clock on Sunday afternoon, having first secured extra invitations for Sarah, Rebecca, Miriam and Eugene. Rosemount had a home match on Saturday, which meant that he would be at Sarah's on Friday evening. He could tell them all then. Just how he was going to break it to them, he wasn't quite sure.

19.00 Friday 4th September 1970. Beethoven Gardens.

Sarah, Miriam, Eugene, Rebecca, Charles and Lionel all sat around the dinner table.

"I've got some news,' Lionel announced as they all started eating their chicken soup.

'Not good timing Lion,' said Eugene. 'Right when we're tucking into the chicken soup. Can't it wait a few minutes, it'll go cold?'

They all held their spoons hovering over their soup and looked at him. He felt himself blushing.

'It'll only take a few seconds' Lionel said. 'But first, you all have to understand that what I'm about to say is in the strictest confidence. It mustn't be spoken about outside of this house until I say it's OK. Understood?'

They all nodded in agreement.

'OK then. I'm leaving Rosemount. Actually, I'm quitting football.' he said.

The soup-spoons went back down onto the table.

Rebecca was the first to speak. 'Why, what are you going to do?'

Lionel had thought long and hard about how he was going to break the news to them and run a suggestion by Jonas. His soon to be new boss had approved the idea. Eugene knew what Lionel was going to say, but he hadn't told Miriam.

'The Prime minister has asked me to work for the government. I'm joining the Home Office.' Lionel said.

Sarah nodded knowingly. She had guessed correctly.

Miriam gasped and looked at Eugene.

'You knew,' she accused him.

Eugene grimaced guiltily.

Rebecca's jaw dropped.

Charles was Sarah's companion. He was in love with Sarah in the 1940's. They were close friends when Solomon went off to the war with the RAF, meeting regularly in a local teashop and he consoled her as she pined for her fiancé. Charles was excluded from signing up for health reasons. He lost her when Solomon returned from the war and he and Sarah married. Sarah was unexpectedly reunited with Charles when Lionel's first record breaking mile run and explosive goal scoring achievements were featured on the television. He was working as a Daily Express reporter. He arrived at their home to ask if he could report on Lionel's career. He gained the family's confidence, (all except for Solomon who didn't entirely trust his motives) and for the past two years had exclusive access to Lionel as he went from event to event and from match to match. Upon hearing Lionel's surprise announcement, he reached for his reporter's notebook but spotting a discreet shake of the head from Sarah he left it in his pocket.

A stunned silence momentarily enveloped the dinner table.

'What about your football, and Rosemount? What will you do?' Miriam asked.

'It's all been taken care of,' Lionel said. 'Gavin Williams's team will sort it out. Look,' he added, 'I've had a great couple of years, achieved more than I could ever have dreamed about. But what I've been asked to do now is far more important and more worthwhile. I can't go into too much detail. All I can do is ask you to trust my judgement.'

'So what do we call you now, 00 Lion?' joked Eugene.

'If I told you that I'd have to kill you.' Lionel said. 'Eat your soup Eugene, before it goes cold.'

'Yes, please, everyone,' Sarah said. 'Eat your dinner. Let's enjoy the meal and we can talk afterwards.'

They nodded and ate in a comfortable silence, which was occasionally broken by smatterings of genial conversation. Unlike before, when Solomon was alive and was seated at the head of the table. Although the family still mourned his passing, they were grateful that they were able to relax knowing that his volcanic temper would not unexpectedly erupt with all hell breaking loose at any moment.

Later, they sat together in the lounge. Charles had left straight after the meal. He'd decided that what he didn't hear, he couldn't write about. What he had heard at the table was a confidence that as a family guest he was privileged to hear. Apart from his relationship with Lionel, he had grown very close to Sarah again. He wasn't prepared to risk damaging his renewed chances of a future with her by breaching that confidence.

Miriam spoke first.

'Eugene, what I don't understand is why you're so happy about this. I thought you enjoyed being part of the El Lion band wagon. No offence Lionel, you understand what I mean.'

'None taken, and I do understand. Eugene please explain.'

'It's simple really. Football is like anything else. Once someone's head has been turned, then they can't apply themselves one hundred percent, and the performance level drops. Then the crowd turns on them, and all the good stuff they've done before gets very quickly and easily forgotten. If Lionel is considering packing it in, he should do it now, while he's at the top, not when he's on the way down.'

'Will it be dangerous?' Rebecca asked. 'What is it exactly that he's asking you to do? I mean after what he saw you do in Germany he made that comment didn't he?'

In Berlin, after Lionel had saved his wife the Prime Minister remarked that if Lionel had been in his protection team his wife might not have been taken in the first place.

'I'm sure I'll be fine Rebecca. I'll have to go through training before they send me anywhere, which they won't do until they're sure I'm ready anyway. Right, I've got a match tomorrow. Come on, if you don't mind I'll walk you home.'

They stood and Lionel walked with Rebecca out of the front door, past his brand-new black MG Midget which still sat idle on the drive. He'd been too busy to take his driving test so he accompanied her on the fifteen-minute walk to her home. They held hands as they walked along in relative silence.

As they approached her house she pulled him to a standstill.

'Promise me you'll be careful.' She pleaded.

'I promise,' he said sincerely.

'They kissed tenderly and held tightly on to each other for a few moments. Then Rebecca walked quickly to her front door, unlocked it, turned, waved and disappeared inside.

As Lionel began the walk home, he tried to focus on his last match which was due to take place the following day. But thoughts of what was about to be yet another new chapter in his relatively short life kept intruding into his mind.

15.00 Saturday 5th September 1970. Rosemount Rovers.

Rosemount were at home to Brownlow United. Always a grudge match, the North London derby game was played with unbridled raw passion. Breakneck pace and crunching tackles were typical features of these games, and today was no exception. They weren't ten minutes into the game before Lionel had been upended twice. Jonas's suggestion that they should put out a covering press release saying that Lionel had suffered a career ending injury during the game might actually prove to be true. What was actually proving true was Eugene's analysis of why Lionel should quit sooner rather than later. He wasn't his usual self. If he was he would have avoided those tackles, instead of being roughly dumped onto his backside.

'Are you OK lad?' Johnny Graves asked as he jogged past him.

'Yeah, sure Johnny, thanks.'

'Watch that Mandela. He's a right hard nut. He won't think twice about taking you out of the game.'

'Yeah thanks, I remember from last season.'

'Well you made him look a bit of a mug then, which is probably why he's tagged you twice already today,'

Half time came and Rosemount, the reigning First Division champions, who weren't playing well found themselves trailing to a stunning strike from Peter Cherry. Lionel had contributed very little.

McPherson didn't hold back in the dressing room. 'What the fuck is wrong with you lot today. They're all over yous. You're bloody lucky you're only one goal down. And where are you today Streat. Buck your ideas up lad or I'll haul your arse off. When you get back out there be first to the ball, and don't waste it when you get it. Spread the play out. They're over-running you in the centre of the park. And Streat, play a bit further forward. You're too close to Graves. Now go on. And remember, you're the bloody champions, not those bastards, so play like it.

McPherson had a well-deserved reputation for his game changing half time rollickings. And today was no exception. Rosemount tore into

Brownlow in the second half, giving them no chance from the first moment the referee blew his whistle to signal the restart. Lionel pushed the ball to Graves who immediately switched it back to Mackan. In a move which had been well-rehearsed on the practice ground, Mackan floated the ball over the Brownlow half back line and between the full backs, where Lionel had sprinted and watching it carefully as it dropped towards him he pivoted and caught it perfectly on the volley with his right foot to steer it ferociously past the goalkeeper and level the score. The supporters were used to seeing this quality of goal from Lionel but even then the cheers lasted for several minutes, and the relief all around the ground was palpable. After a brace of typical poacher's goals from Graves, which were sandwiched by Lionel's rocket header from a corner, Rosemount ran out winners by four goals to one. Lionel, on instructions from Jonas walked off the pitch with a heavy limp.

11.00 Sunday 6th September 1970. Johnny Graves's digs.

'Johnny, can I have a word,'
'Sure Lion, what's up Lionel? How's the knee?'
'It's fine, sit down, please, it's important.'
'Sounds ominous.'
'It is Johnny, I'm not coming back to the club. I won't be playing for them again.'
'What are you talking about? Listen, Lion, if it's because of the way the gaffer spoke to you at half time, take no bloody notice. You should be used to it by now. We've all experienced it and you can't argue it did the trick didn't it? Look at what we did to them in the second half.'
'No, it's not that Johnny. I've been offered a job somewhere else.'
Johnny's face went white.
'You're going to another club? You can't. How could you do that? You're a Rosemount man. You've said so yourself, you've been a fan since you were a kid. Unless that was all bullshit. And anyway you've got a contract.'
'Johnny, it's a secret. It's not in football. But you can't tell anyone Not even Dan. I'm only telling

you out of respect for our friendship and how you've helped me. I'm going to work for the British Government.'

Graves sat there staring at Lionel, completely stupefied, his jaw hanging open.

'Fuck me sideways, inside and out. You're not kidding me are you?'

'No I'm not. The club is going to get a phone call from the Prime Minister's office in the morning. They're going to agree a cover story about me having a serious injury and sort out my contract. If McPherson asks you anything please say you don't know and that I didn't stay with you tonight. I'm moving back home now anyway. I'm going to Downing Street this afternoon.'

The penny suddenly dropped.

'Hold on, did you say Downing Street? This is to do with what went on in Germany after the final isn't it?'

'I can't answer that, Johnny, and you have to promise that you won't say anything.'

Graves could see that Lionel's mind was made up.

'OK, Lion, I promise. Just call me Sergeant Shultz. I know nothing,' he said putting on a comic German accent, 'but I'm going to miss you,' he said, standing up. 'You do realise that McPherson is going to blow his bloody top don't you? I hope it's worth it and it works out for you.'

'I know, Johnny, but I have to do this, and I'm sure it will be worth it.'

'I hope you're right. Come on, I'll help you pack up your gear and run you to your mother's place.'

13.50 Sunday 6th September 1970. Beethoven Gardens.

At one fifty, the sleek Daimler limousine pulled up outside the smart semi-detached house in Beethoven Gardens. The uniformed driver dressed in smart navy livery knocked on the door and the family filed out and climbed into the back of the car. An hour later Basil Armstrong met them at the door of 10 Downing Street. He escorted them through to a large room, where Gavin and Edith Williams were talking with a stern looking tall blonde-haired clean-shaven man in a black three-piece suit and knitted red tie, Armstrong introduced him to Lionel as Louis Schneider, the German Ambassador.

'Thank you for your service to my country,' he said with a thick accent. 'I am told that you showed a great deal of bravery, almost verging on the foolhardy.'

Lionel wasn't sure how to react to what he sensed was a back-handed compliment, but he was saved by Edith Williams.

'Lionel was indeed very brave Louis. I might not be here today if it wasn't for him. Thank you again Lionel.'

'It was my pleasure Mrs Williams.'

'Shall we get on with things?' Gavin Williams said.

'Good idea, Prime Minister,' said Schneider. I have to get back to the embassy for a meeting.

'Please be seated everyone,' called out Basil Armstrong.

Gavin and Edith Williams sat in the front row. Gavin Williams signaled to Lionel to sit next to him.

Armstrong sat with the family in the row behind. Also in the room were a few diplomats and civil servants, who Lionel had no doubt he would be meeting in due course.

Harold Jonas entered the room and went and sat next to Armstrong.

Gavin Williams stood up and walked to the lectern, which was positioned in front of the rows of chairs.

After a few brief words of welcome he called upon Schneider to present Lionel with a specially commissioned medal, the first peacetime medal for bravery which the German government had awarded to a non-German civilian. An honour indeed. Schneider said all the right things. He even tried to crack a joke about England's lucky victory in the World Cup final, which was greeted by a ripple of polite laughter.

Then Gavin Williams returned to the lectern. This time he spoke for a little longer. He said how Lionel represented a new generation of brave British youth. How he had acted without any thought for his own safety and how the future of Britain would surely be safe in the hands of him and his contemporaries. He called Lionel forward again to receive his medal, and Edith Williams to present it to him. Lionel shook both of their hands and sat down. Polite applause echoed around the room.

Heavy purple velvet drapes were pulled back to reveal a sumptuous cream tea and Basil Armstrong invited everyone to help themselves. As Lionel was about to move forward Harold Jonas took hold of his arm.

'Hang back a moment lad would you?'

Gavin Williams came over to join them.

'Congratulations Mister Streat,'

'Thank you sir, but this was all very unnecessary.'

'As it happens, it wasn't. Anyway that's not what I meant. I'm congratulating you because I understand you've agreed to join Mister Jonas's team. Which means you'll be part of the team responsible for looking after me and my wife. After that fiasco in Berlin I couldn't be happier. You see, we're off to Russia in three months' time and I want you to come along. Harold, make sure he's trained up by then please would you. Now come along Lionel I want you to meet a few people.'

With that he took Lionel by the arm and steered him away leaving Harold Jonas standing there on his own with a look of incredulity on his face.

09.00 Monday 7th September 1970. Rosemount Rovers.

Basil Armstrong arrived unannounced at the Rosemount chairman's office at nine o'clock and waited for him to arrive, which he did at nine-thirty. Clive Stimpson, dressed in an expensive navy mohair suit, short, and fat with ruddy skin and thinning white hair plopped himself down in the plush leather chair behind his ornate walnut desk. Not being a man to mince his words he asked Armstrong straight out what he wanted. Armstrong responded in kind, informing Stimpson that Lionel would be working for the government with immediate effect. He didn't say in what capacity. He told him firmly what the club were to announce and proposed a compensation package. Stimpson was a sensible and astute businessman. Knowing when he was beaten and encouraged by the size of the compensation amount he agreed without too much protest. The meeting was over in less than fifteen minutes and Armstrong stood and strode out of Stimpson's office. Stimpson was left shell-shocked and in no doubt what would happen if anything other than what he had agreed would be released in the press was ever disclosed. He summoned his chauffer and drove straight to the training ground. He marched into Willie McPherson's ramshackle office, waving his hand in front of his face to signal his distaste at the smell of the stale cigarettes. He proceeded to inform the manager of what had taken place, and that they would be putting out a press release saying that Lionel had been injured in the game on Saturday and it was unlikely that he would ever play again. Stimpson didn't tell McPherson why, or about Armstrong's visit. Only that he must never reveal anything to anyone other than what he was told and what was going to appear in the newspapers. If he did he would lose his job immediately. He left McPherson sitting there seething and escaped out into the fresh air. He didn't go back to the club, he instructed the chauffeur to take him home and wait outside while he had a shower and a change of clothes.

As soon as he was alone McPherson slammed his fist on the desk. He went to the door, flung it open and screamed for Graves and Mackan to come in. He lit another cigarette while he waited for them.

'How was Streat when you saw him last?' he fired at Johnny.

Johnny looked at Mackan, who of course knew nothing, only that Lionel hadn't shown up that morning. When he'd asked Johnny if he knew anything all Johnny had said was that he didn't and that Lionel hadn't stayed with him the night before.

'Well I haven't seen him since yesterday morning boss. He was hobbling a bit but it didn't look like anything serious. Why, what's going on?'

'I don't fucking know and that's the truth of it. The Chairman has just been to see me.'

'Yeah, we saw his flying visit,' Mackan said.

'Well why he knew before me I've got no idea but Lionel isn't going to be playing anymore. He's packed it in, says he's got an injury to his knee and it's finished his career.'

'That's bollocks!' shouted Mackan.

Johnny remained silent.

'Well it probably is, and I'm as sick as a parrot about it. But I've been told in no uncertain terms to suck it up, swallow it and get on with it. And so must you and the boys. I've said before that no-one is bigger than this club. So we'll just have to move on and prove it. Let me have your thoughts during the week about who we can draft into the first eleven as a replacement. Go on the pair of you. Tell the lads. I'll be out soon.'

The two players walked out to join the rest of the squad for training.

'You really knew nothing about this Johnny?' asked Don.

'Not a word, until just now.' said Johnny innocently. 'You're the club captain. You tell the boys.'

'Yeah thanks mate.' Don replied.

'Gather round lads,' he called out as they approached the training pitch. 'I've got some news for you that you're not going to believe, or like very much.'

Harold Jonas's secretary showed Lionel into his office.

'Ah, Streat, welcome,' he said. Are you ready to commence your training?'

'Yes sir'.

'Fine, there is a lot for you to learn.'

'I'm a quick learner sir.'

'Yes I know all about your education, your exam results and all that, but you can't learn everything that you have to know from any manuals.'

'I understand.'

'Good,' Jonas said. 'First there's some documentation you have to sign. Official Secrets Act and some other boring stuff. You appreciate that you can't even tell your wife what goes on here. As far as she's concerned you're a pen pusher, an analyst, and that's all.'

Lionel laughed, 'I'm not married sir.'

'Ok, yes of course, I was forgetting your age. Well you will be one day. So until then it's your darling mummy and everybody else you can't say a word to. If you do it's a thing called treason. We'll leave it at that. So, I'm putting you with Captain Arnold Courtenay. He's an experienced senior training officer in the SAS, and he'll show you the ropes, but I'm warning you it will be pretty intensive. Remember what the PM said. He wants you ready for Russia in three months, and if anybody can have you ready in time, it's him,.'

'I'll be ready sir.'

'Let's hope so.'

There was a knock on the door.

'Come,' called Jonas.

A six foot plus soldier in army fatigues and a black beret marched briskly into the room. He was tanned, and his bare arms rippled with thick rope-like muscle. He looked like he was in his forties, but because of the life he led he could well have been younger.

'Ah,' said Jonas. 'Talk of the devil and in he walks. Lionel Streat, meet Captain Courtenay. One of the British Army's toughest soldiers.

To Lionel's surprise Courtenay saluted Jonas. Then he turned and looked him up and down as if appraising him. With a smug sneer on his weathered and lined face he said, 'So you're El

Lion eh? I've heard all about you lad. I even cheered you on in the football. You saved the P.M.'s wife's bacon to boot. Well done and all that.'

He spoke with a deep gravelly voice and had a strong Scottish accent. It reminded Lionel of Willie McPherson.

'But that's all got to be put behind you now my lad. That's all history. Your life starts again today. I've been asked to get you up to scratch in three months. It usually takes the best recruits six, and only a handful of 'em make the grade. Even mine, and I'm the best trainer there is. The sheer hell of it breaks the rest. Do you think you've got the mettle to get through it? You'll have my undivided attention, because everything will be one to one, just you and me. So we'll both have to match up to the challenge. I've got to get you ready, and you've got to be ready. Think carefully before you answer. Engage your brain before you engage your mouth. Because you might think that you're fit, but let me tell you this my son, until you've trained with me on the Brecon Beacons you haven't got the faintest idea what fitness and endurance is.'

'Is your lecture over now Captain Courtenay?' Jonas asked with an impatient sigh.

Jonas, a retired SAS Major, still outranked Courtenay. The Captain clicked his heels together smartly, trying his best to hide his anger at being spoken to like that in front of a new recruit.

'Yes sir, it is sir. Just letting the boy here know what he's letting himself in for sir.'

'Good, so what's your answer Streat? Do you think you have what it takes?' Lionel didn't hesitate. He looked Courtenay square in the eye.

'Let's do it then,' he said.

'Good man,' said Courtenay. 'Let's go.'

05.00 Tuesday 8th December. 1970 Brecon Beacons.

Lionel tried his hardest not to look too self-satisfied as he turned and waited for Captain Courtenay to catch him up as they began the last stretch of the sixteen-mile Brecon Beacons march. All the way through the hike Lionel had matched the Captain stride for stride, until it was the recruit who was leading the way and pushing the trainer to keep up through the freezing snow.

"What's your real fucking name Streat, Clark fucking Kent?' Gasped Courtenay as he caught Lionel up. 'How the hell are you managing to do this? In all my years I've never seen anything like it. You're not fucking human.'

Lionel smiled politely as they made it back to base camp. Training was over. The march had been the final exercise in their arduous three-month schedule. Lionel had impressed all the way through, never shirking from any of the exercises and the two men had bonded well. Courtenay realised from day one that Lionel was no pushover. Every time he pushed his new recruit a bit harder Lionel responded and was up to the challenge. The only time he had hesitated was at pistol and rifle training.

'You may not like the idea Streat, but if you can't use one of these, you'll be about as much use to the PM as a chocolate teapot. If some mad bastard is threatening the life of someone you are sworn to protect you take the fucker out, no questions asked.'

'What about if he hasn't got a gun?' Lionel asked innocently.

'Come on lad, don't you remember what I told you on the very first day when I was explaining how to recognise a threat? You might not see a gun, but it doesn't mean that he hasn't got one. What if he's got a machete hidden, or an explosive device?'

Lionel didn't answer. He went through the firearm training and once again impressed his tutor, who by now knew not to be surprised when his student excelled.

The helicopter was waiting to take them back to barracks. They sat facing each other. The pilot's jaw dropped when he recognized the younger of his passengers, but he knew better than to say anything.

'So,' Courtenay said as they climbed aboard, 'what they wrote about you in the newspapers was true then wasn't it? I suppose it had to be for you to do what you did in the Olympics and in the World Cup, not to mention after the bloody game!'

It was more of a statement than a question.

Lionel nodded. 'One kick in the head and my whole life changed,' he said.

Lionel was referring to the incident which had triggered his metamorphosis from a puny sixteen-year-old little boy to a much larger, stronger and abler teenager. Being so small Lionel was regularly bullied and suffered with the nickname weed. That very morning he'd been beaten up in the classroom by two boys, Geoff Cannon and Dave Ruby for being made a school prefect. During a school rugby game later that day, Mickey Steele, a friend of Cannon's and Ruby's had deliberately kicked Lionel in the back of the head as he bravely lay on the ground shielding the ball. When Lionel stood up he had grown to be almost unrecognisable. He shoved Steele so hard that he landed several feet away. The games master awarded Lionel's team a penalty and instructed Lionel to take it. With no apparent effort he kicked the rugby ball the length of the pitch through the centre of the posts, drawing cheers from his team-mates and expletives from Frank Townshend, the games master!

The other teacher, Rod Baines, was the senior games teacher and was overseeing a football match on the adjacent pitch. He came over to see what all the fuss was about. He was protective of Lionel and responsible for him becoming a prefect. He instructed Lionel to retake the kick, which he did with exactly the same result, except that this time the ball travelled further and nearly ended up in the road 150 yards away, which brought more cheers from the boys, and more expletives from Townshend.

Baines sent the boys on a run, thinking it would calm things down. It didn't. The run was just about a mile long, around the perimeter of the sports fields. It should have taken the boys around six minutes. Lionel started about thirty seconds after them, overtook them all and finished in under three minutes forty-five seconds. Cannon and Ruby accused him of cheating. Lionel challenged them, and Steele to a boxing match. As much as Rod Baines tried to dissuade him he was determined and strode off to the gym to wait for them.

When they arrived he handed each of the three of them a pair boxing gloves. He wanted to take them all on at once, and there was no dissuading him. Cannon and Ruby relished the opportunity. Steele was not so sure. Luckily for him he made the right choice and held back. Cannon shaped to take a swing at Lionel but before he'd raised his arm he was floored by a blow to his stomach, as was Ruby a second later. Steele, seeing what had happened to his friends declined to get involved and skulked away.

Everyone was stunned, and even more so when twenty minutes later Baines took Lionel back to the football pitch where he fired half a dozen shots past the teacher and into the goal, before he had even had a chance to move a muscle.

That evening Baines made a call to a contact he had and the next day, in front of BBC cameras

Lionel repeated the run in an even better time. He then played in a school football match and scored goals good enough to grace the professional game. His amazing career was launched to the nation in a matter of twenty-four hours.

Now, two years later, on the Brecon Beacons, seeing Lionel performing at the same incredible level, Courtenay said 'Well, I've never said this to anyone in my charge before, and if you ever repeat it I'll deny having said it.'

Lionel looked up into the smiling face of the man who had put him through three of the hardest months he had ever endured.

'It's been a privilege to work with you. I can see why they call you El Lion now. I've enjoyed every minute.' He extended his hand to Lionel who shook it gratefully.

'So have I sir. So have I. Thank you for getting me through it.'

'It's been a pleasure. You just make sure you keep our Prime Minister safe and it will have been worth it. But I've got a feeling it's not going to end for you there. I see bigger things for you. I think you're going to be helping to keep this whole country safe, not just the wanker and his wife in 10 Downing Street.'

Lionel laughed out loud.

Courtenay smiled pensively and as the helicopter began its bumpy way back to London they both looked out of the sides and down at the Black Mountains and the Welsh countryside.

11.00 Wednesday 15th December 1970. Moscow.

The aeroplane bearing Gavin and Edith Williams and their party of ten touched down at Domodedovo Airport Moscow. It taxied carefully along the icy tarmac as it made its approach to the terminal. A fleet of four identical large black SUVs drove up to meet it. Each vehicle had two dour looking burly Russians in the front. They were all dressed in heavy woolen coats and ushanka-hats to protect against the severe cold from the sudden onset of the early Russian winter.

As the entourage made its way down the staircase from the plane every one of them shivered as the biting wind chilled them and they pulled up their collars. Jonas led the way and at the foot of the stairs he split them. He directed four of the protection team to split and go two into the front and two into the fourth suburban. He went with Gavin Williams and one other guard in the second vehicle and he put Lionel in the third with Edith Williams and the last of the guards. The cars drove them over to the diplomatic suite, where Harold Jonas took the paperwork to be checked by a stern faced official. The official left him standing there while he came out and took his time peering into every window of each car while he deliberated over each piece of documentation. He stared long and hard at Gavin Williams, the expression on his face indicating that he was enjoying winding up the British Prime Minister. Finally satisfied he marched back into the building. A few minutes later Jonas strode briskly back out and the cars left the airport to make the hour-long journey, fifty miles down the A105 to the British Embassy on Smolenskaya Naberezhnaya in central Moscow. Fifty-five minutes later two motorcycle policemen joined the procession as it began the long sweeping turn around the Lotte Plaza to guide them along the approach to Protochny, which had been closed to keep it clear for them so it was empty of pedestrians and traffic. When they were only a few minutes away from the embassy, a rocket soared between two tall buildings and struck the first car which left the ground in a roaring pyre and landed fifty feet away. The two motorcycles and riders were blown to pieces. They and the occupants of the suburban didn't stand a chance. In the vehicle behind Gavin William's driver shouted '*trakhni menya*' and stamped hard on the brake, throwing his passengers backwards and then forwards as the seatbelts locked and held them on their seats.

'Everybody down,' yelled Jonas.

'That will do us a lot of good when another rocket hits us,' said Williams.

'There won't be any more rockets,' said Jonas, drawing his pistol. 'That one was to stop us. I doubt if they want to kill you. More likely they want to grab you, which means they'll be coming for you soon.'

In the third car Lionel and his team-mate had already pulled Edith Williams to the floor.

'Sorry for the rough treatment Mrs Williams,' he said, but it's for your own safety.'

'I understand' she said, remarkably calmly. 'It looks like you've got to save me again Lionel doesn't it.'

In the vehicle behind, the two protection team men peered cautiously over the sill of their car doors, guns at the ready, waiting for the opportunity to see what was going to happen next.

There were few seconds of eerie silence, apart from the crackling of the flames from the nearby remains of the burning SUV. Suddenly a black van raced around the corner from the opposite direction and screeched to a halt twenty yards away. The rear doors flew open and three men in balaclavas and fatigues and carrying AK47 rifles jumped out and started firing at the three remaining cars, strafing them as they calmly walked towards them. But the armour reinforced bodywork and glass did its job and held.

'Where's the local police?' Lionel asked his colleague.

'Probably hiding around the corner shitting their pants, excuse me Mrs Williams.' Came the reply.

'Don't worry young man, you're probably absolutely right,' she said wryly, still prone on the floor of the car.

Then they stopped firing as suddenly as they had started. One of the gunmen, who Jonas assumed was the leader came up closer and gestured to his driver, waving the barrel of his machine gun. The driver and his companion stepped out of the car. The gunman pointed to the rear passenger door. The driver looked at the door and back at the gunman. He knew what the gunman wanted, which was to open the door to make it easier for him to get to the passengers. He looked again back at the door and through the window. Jonas had his pistol pointed directly at him. The Russian knew from Jonas's fierce expression that if he opened that door he wouldn't live to enjoy his next plate of caviar. Jonas immediately got on the radio to his team members.

'Don't let the drivers open the fucking doors. If you think they are going to, shoot the bastards. Keep these channels open'

The unanimous response immediately came back, 'Roger that,' and in the middle suburban without hesitation Lionel's colleague rammed his pistol into the back of the driver's head and said, 'do you both speak English?' Seeing them both nod he said, 'great, both of you, open your windows a crack and drop your guns outside the car. If you even twitch a millimeter towards the back I will shoot you both dead. Then close your windows back up and keep your hands in front of you. If either of you moves a finger towards the doors I will still not hesitate to shoot you both dead.' Another nod.

'Don't worry,' the driver's companion said in a gruff voice. 'They not Russian. If they Russian we would know about it. They kill you, then they kill us as well.'

'Well we're not taking any chances, do it, now'.

Then they did exactly as they were told. Their windows buzzed quietly down a little and their pistols clattered on to the floor outside the car. The windows buzzed closed again and they laid their hands in their laps.

'Good move,' whispered Jonas. 'Brogan, do the same.'

In the back vehicle both Brogan and the other Englishman trained their guns on the Russians in the front. Nothing more needed to be said. With the radio channel open everything that was said was being heard. They got the message loud and clear, saw their fellow countrymen in the car in front comply, dropped their own guns out of the car and placed their hands in their laps.

The gunman was becoming more and more frustrated.

'Open the door,' he called out to the driver in heavily accented English

'Why don't you open it?' the other Russian said. He hadn't seen the look that Jonas had given his compatriot.

'Because the bastard Englishman will shoot me,' he said in Russian, hoping the gunman wouldn't understand.

The gunman moved closer, 'Open it he said.'

The Russian still didn't move. The AK47 spat out five bullets in rapid succession and the top half of the Russian driver's head exploded in a mass of blood mangled body parts. The other Russian tried to run, but he was fat and slow, and his body was decimated in another burst of gunfire.

The gunman walked up to the car. Smoke curled from the muzzle of his AK47. Harold Jonas and the other protection team guard sat either side of Gavin Williams. All three men stared defiantly out of the window. The other two gunmen positioned themselves, one at each of the two rear SUVs.

The gunman looked through the window at Gavin Williams and laughed. He held up a two-way radio and spoke into it. He'd hacked into their frequency and they could hear him inside the car.

'I don't really want you, Mister British Prime Minister Williams,' he sneered. If I did my rocket would have taken out your car, not the other one. I want El Lion. Tell him to come to me, otherwise I will kill every one of you, including your wife.'

'Why, what do you want with him?' Jonas called out.

'He caused me a lot of embarrassment in Berlin, not to mention the inconvenience. My brother was one of those men he helped the Germans to apprehend. So I want you to give him to me. I will teach him a lesson. I will make him suffer. And then I will give him back to you, in exchange for my brother.'

'You know we can't do that.' Jonas said

'Oh but I know that you can, and I know that you will.' The gunman glanced back towards the van. The rear doors opened again, to reveal a third terrorist holding a rocket launcher.

'No doubt he is in the car with Mrs Williams. Which means that he is in the vehicle behind yours. So who is in the vehicle at the back? Shall we take that one out first?'

Before anyone could answer, Lionel spoke. His voice was calm, but his tone was firm.

'Wait. I'm coming out. Don't kill anybody else.'

'Stay where you are Streat,' Jonas said. 'Your job is to protect Mrs Williams. You're can't do that if you're dead.'

'If he doesn't come out, your car will be the next one to eat a rocket,' said the gunman.' The guy holding the rocket launcher rotated to aim it squarely at the Prime Minister's SUV.

Edith Williams began to panic. 'Oh my God. What do we do, what do we do?.'

'Stay calm, please Edith,' Gavin Williams called to her.

'Yes Edith, stay calm' the gunman mimicked. 'As soon as El Lion comes out you can all go on your way.'

From the other end of the road three police cars suddenly appeared, sirens blaring.

The rocket launcher coughed, the missile landed squarely on the lead car and it was vapourised. Policemen poured out of the other two cars and ran for cover.

In the back of the van the guy loaded another rocket and aimed it back at Gavin Williams's car.

Lionel held the mute button down on the two-way radio. 'Listen,' he said to Ed Black, the team member with him and Edith Williams. 'I'm going to have to go otherwise that rocket launcher is going to take out the Prime Minister. Sorry to be blunt Mrs Williams but that's the way it looks.'

All Edith Williams could do was nod.

'When I step out of the car, can you cover me?' Lionel asked Black.

'Sure, but I hope you know what you're doing.'

'Stay down Mrs Williams,' Lionel said as he opened the door and slowly edged out. Black slid along the seat and pointed his pistol through the door jamb.

'Very good El Lion,' The gunman said, keep walking this way please.' As Lionel walked towards him the two other terrorists followed behind him.

'What the hell is he doing?' Jonas spluttered. 'I told him to stay in the car.'

'That kids got balls, I'll say that for him,' Brogan said as he opened his door and took cover behind it.

Brogan and Black had both terrorists who were behind Lionel in their sights.

'You're just a boy,' the gunman said to Lionel as he got closer. 'A boy doing a man's work. Does your mother know that you are out? And what is your government thinking giving you the Prime Minister's wife to …..'

He didn't finish his sentence. In a flash, so fast that the gunman didn't have a chance to take any evasive action, Lionel threw himself forward, and grabbing the barrel of the rifle with his right hand he dropped down and swept his feet away from under him. As the gunman landed heavily on the tarmac, Lionel punched him on the side of his head with his left hand rendering him unconscious. It was so quick that no-one had an opportunity to react. And before the other terrorists could move Black and

Brogan had put bullets into the back of their heads.

Lionel swivelled on the floor with the AK47 and fired a round into the back of the van and the guy with the rocket launcher was killed instantly.

It was over.

Everyone stepped out of the cars.

From the last car the driver said to Brogan.

'Who is that fucking guy?'

'That my Russian friend is El Lion.'

'You can relax now Mrs Williams,' Ed Black said as he helped her back up on to the seat.

'Is my husband all right?' she asked.

'Yes, he's safe.'

'And Lionel, what about Lionel.'

'El Lion is safe as well,' he assured her.

The Russian police, who had been cowering at the other end of the road ran forward. They checked the bodies of the dead terrorists, and that there was no-one else in the van. Apart from the man who had been launching the rockets it was empty. He must have also been the driver.

While the police were handcuffing the gunman, who was still unconscious, Harold Jonas and Gavin Williams stepped up behind Lionel, who was standing with his head bowed. The AK47 hung loosely in his hand. He hadn't moved since he had fired it into the van.

Realising that it was Lionel's first kill, Jonas, in a rare moment of sensitivity, put his hand on Lionel's shoulder.

'Are you OK lad?'

Lionel looked up. His face was pale, but there was steel in his eyes.

'Yes sir. Thank you, I'm fine,' he said quietly.

'You realise that if you hadn't done what you did we would probably all be dead by now. My word, when Captain Courtenay reported to me you were something special, I didn't realise quite how right he was. Just one thing to bear in mind though lad.'

'What's that sir?'

Jonas leaned closer to Lionel and whispered into his ear. 'You've got away with it this time lad, but don't disobey my fucking instructions again!'

Lionel lifted his head and saw that Jonas had a playful grin on his face.

'No sir, I won't.'

From behind them Gavin Williams, who had Stone, the other protection team guard who had been in his car standing next to him said, 'It looks like I've got to thank you again Lionel. It makes me all the more pleased now that I insisted that you came on this trip. Thank you Harold for agreeing to arrange it. And pass my thanks to Courtenay as well.'

'And mine,' said Edith Williams, who had walked to join them. Black and Brogan and the last member of the protection team from Brogan's SUV were with her.

A plain clothed Russian policeman who was in one of the three police cars that the rocket launcher had fired at walked briskly down from further down the street and came over to speak to them.

'Who is Mister Jonas?' he asked officiously.

Harold Jonas stepped forward. 'I am.' he said. 'Who are you?'

'I am Lieutenant Kuznetsova. I was dispatched here with my men as soon as we heard that the terrorists had attacked you.' He surveyed the carnage. 'I am very sorry that it has happened in my country. You should be aware that you may still not be safe. So if you would please immediately get back into your vehicles we will escort you to your embassy.'

Jonas looked at Gavin Williams, who shook his head vigorously.

'No thank you.'

'What do you mean?'

'We've lost good men here this afternoon. So have you. But that was because your security measures were seriously lacking. You should have been escorting us all the way from the airport. Not two bloody motorcycles once we were practically here. What were your superiors thinking of? So, we are not going to the embassy. We will leave that for another occasion. We are going home. Kindly escort us back to the airport instead. Radio those superiors of yours and ask them to arrange for our plane to be ready.'

The lieutenant raised his eyebrows and looked at Gavin Williams as if requesting his confirmation. Williams said sharply, 'You heard what Mister Jonas said. Please do what he asked without delay.'

Kuznetsova nodded and called out a few instructions to his men in Russian.

They all got quickly back into their vehicles and made their way to Domodedovo airport.

Wednesday 12th July 1995. Willesden Cemetery.

On what had earlier been an unusually dull afternoon for the time of year, Lionel stood staring as Sarah's coffin was lowered into her freshly dug grave. The rain had stopped only an hour ago, and the grey clouds had parted to let through golden summer sunbeams.

Miriam squeezed his hand tightly as the tears ran freely down his cheeks. She glanced up towards the heavens.

'You see Lionel,' she said, 'the sun always shines on the righteous, and its shining for mum now.'

'I know,' he said. 'she was an angel during her lifetime. She always did her best to protect us from dad. And now, well, she'll still be our guardian angel, only now it will be from heaven.'

They hugged and turned to Rebecca, who stood just behind him with their three children. Eugene was next to her with his and Miriam's two girls. Behind them was Charles, and a host of family and friends. Sarah hadn't married Charles, but they had spent twenty-five happy years together. Charles's kind and generous personality had proved very popular with everybody who was close to Sarah, and who had known the torment she had endured during her marriage to Solomon. But being old fashioned she had declined marriage, and they hadn't lived together. Having succumbed to cancer, she was now laid to rest alongside her husband. Charles was devastated, but nonetheless grateful for the time that he had with Sarah.

The Rabbi recited the dirge of the memorial prayers, and then everyone traipsed sadly back to the chapel for the concluding part of the service.

As people came up to offer Lionel their condolences he politely avoided any questions about how he was or what he was doing. He was an enigma, having disappeared almost overnight from the public scene some twenty-five years ago. All that remained of those days was the book he had been contracted to finish. Rumours abounded about his work for the government, but because his activities were shrouded in secrecy, that was all that they were. Just rumours. He and Rebecca had three children, two boys and a girl. All of them were young adults now, but they didn't know what their father's work really entailed. As far as they were concerned he was once a world-famous sportsman who was now a boring Civil Servant. They accepted that he had to spend long periods away and were blissfully ignorant of the peril he put himself in nearly every day. As was everybody, apart from Rebecca. And that was how Lionel had always preferred it to stay. Rebecca agreed with him that what their children didn't know, they couldn't worry about. They didn't want their children, their siblings or parents to spend every day worrying that Lionel might not come home, or that when he did it might be in a body bag.

After the service the family and friends went back to the house in Beethoven Gardens for the start of the *shiva* week. Despite the pleas from her children and Charles, Sarah had refused to move home and she remained there until she died.

By ten o'clock that night, apart from Lionel, Rebecca, Miriam, Eugene and Charles, the house was finally empty. The rest of the week went by in a blur.

A week after the *shiva,* Lionel and Miriam met back at the house to go through some of Sarah's personal effects and to start putting her affairs in order. Both of them had busy work schedules and time was at a premium. They were going through some old papers they had found in a drawer in Sarah's dressing table. Among them was a parchment envelope, with "Solomon Streat" written on it in a neat italic script, with what looked like could even have been a quill. Inside it was their father's birth certificate, and his parent's marriage certificate.

'Wow,' said Lionel. 'Have you seen these before?'

'No, never,' said Miriam. 'Mum and dad must have put them away after they got married. That was probably the last time they needed them.'

Lionel carefully unfolded the certificates and read them. The marriage certificate immediately caught his attention. In fading writing it detailed that in 1921 Isaac Streat had married Alexandria Weiss. He had seen the name Weiss recently, somewhere in an office communication. He instantly recalled the complete text and in his mind scanned to the relevant section. It was a few days before his mother had passed away. Nathan Weiss had just been promoted to the Assistant Director of the CIA, at only thirty years old, the youngest in its history.

'Look at this Mirrie,' he said passing it to her.

'What am I looking at?'

'We may have found a relative we didn't know we had. Nathan Weiss, in America.'

'Come on Lionel, it's a bit of a long shot.'

'Not really, Weiss isn't that much of a common name. It's probably been shortened from something longer, making it uncommon enough that there might be a connection. I'll put out a feeler. Wouldn't you like to know if we've got a blood relative across the pond?'

'I suppose so.' Miriam said, without too much enthusiasm.

Lionel slid the certificates carefully back in the envelope and they continued the morbid task of going through their recently departed mother's personal effects.

Noon, Monday 31st July 1995. Westminster.

Lionel, just back from compassionate leave sat at his desk in his office overlooking the Thames. Over the last twenty-five years he had come to be regarded as one of MI5's best agents, and as a reward he had been given his own team and a plush office from which to run his operations. Marvelling at how email had sped up worldwide communication, he composed a message to Nathan Weiss in Washington. It was still only seven o'clock there, but if Nathan wasn't already at his desk, he would find it waiting for him as soon as he arrived.

During the previous week Lionel had managed to track down David Lushman, the member of the GB athletics team he had befriended in the 1968 Olympics. At that time genealogy was a hobby of David's and as a favour to Lionel he had traced Sharon Berman's history. Sharon was a school friend of Lionel's but Lionel's father was convinced that she was German, and because of his bigotry he was making Lionel's life a misery over their friendship. David had discovered that Sharon's family were Polish, and Lionel had always been grateful to him for it. When Lionel re-established contact with David, his hobby had grown so much that it was now a successful business tracing ancestral lineages and he was pleased to help. Using the latest specialist software packages which he had at his disposal he managed to establish the link between the Weiss and the Streat families and he emailed the details to Lionel.

Lionel was amazed that a wild hunch had actually proved correct.

'Thanks David,' he replied, 'once again you've come up trumps.'

Lionel's email to Nathan simply said, "Nathan, first, congratulations on your recent promotion. Secondly, I have found some information which proves that we are related. When you have a few spare minutes, perhaps call me for a chat."

Lionel typed in his secure private number and pressed send, watching the message disappear from his screen to miraculously travel the three and half thousand miles across the ether to Washington.

Then returning to work mode, Lionel buried himself in the files which had built up during his absence.

An hour later, his private line rang. It was Nathan.

They greeted each other warmly, and after a brief introductions Lionel said, 'Nathan, I hope you don't mind, but after finding my grandparents marriage certificate I've looked into our family tree, and believe it or not we are actually first cousins.'

'Mind, why on earth would I mind? Since I got your email I did some digging on my own and I found that I'm related to El Lion, the man who still holds the Olympic 1500 meters record, and scored the winning goal in the World Cup Final. That's incredible. Not to mention you're one of the best agents in British intelligence. You understand I would have to know that as well right? Wait till my wife hears.'

'As you rightly said Nathan, not to mention that, especially not to your wife. And I'm related to the Assistant Director of the CIA. That's not too shabby either.'

'Doesn't compare, Lionel. Hey, listen, why don't you come over and visit? You can meet Abbey and bring your wife too.'

'Thanks, I'd love to, but it's a bit difficult Nathan, I've just come back off compassionate leave. My mother passed away a few weeks ago.'

'Oh. I'm sorry, that's one thing I didn't know. My condolences. Still, you're senior enough over there and anyway I'm sure you must be due some time. We've got a retirement party coming up in a few months. Mike riley, the police inspector I worked with on the Kirkpatrick fiasco. We became quite close. I'd love to introduce you to him and some of our friends. Just as a sporting hero, nothing else. They'd be delighted to meet you. And you can stay with us. Come on man, it'll be great.'

'OK Nathan, I'm convinced. Let me speak to Rebecca. I'll set it up. When do you have in mind?'

'Good man. The party's not for a couple of months and I've got some time booked off then as well. So you've got plenty of time to make arrangements. OK? Call me and let me know.'

'Will do,' said Lionel. 'Thanks, I'll be in touch, ... bye cousin.'

Separated by three thousand six hundred odd

miles, and both men looking forward to being reunited, Nathan smiled and hung up in Washington, while in London, Lionel also smiled, hung up and went back to going through his files.

That evening over dinner Lionel excitedly recounted the conversation to Rebecca. Later, after the table was cleared, he grabbed an atlas from the bookcase and together they planned how they would spend the time travelling across the United States. Where they would go sightseeing and where their stopovers would be. Of course they could not have been aware that events during those coming weeks would change their lives forever.

10pm Saturday 8th July 1995. Lake Michigan, Chicago.

A lone figure crawled out of the reeds and along the undergrowth, making his way cautiously up the bank, stopping every few yards to make sure that he couldn't be seen.

He lay down, exhausted, and shivering, rubbing his arms and legs to try to generate some warmth back into them.

During his tenure in Vietnam he had learned how to endure the toughest conditions. Even though it was twenty years ago he could instantly call upon the endurance skills he had mastered and his survival instinct was still as strong as it ever was.

His name was Jake Barclay, and he was on the run. He was a rouge CIA agent, who had double crossed his boss, the Director, Miles Kirkpatrick. Barclay had found out that Kirkpatrick was planning to destroy the formula for a cure for cancer that the Chicago Cancer clinic was close to discovering. Kirkpatrick has sent him to Chicago to investigate how close the clinic actually was to finding the cure. It transpired that the reason Kirkpatrick wanted to destroy the cure was because he had at his disposal a poison which would spawn cancer cells in human beings, and he planned to sell it on the black market. A cure would render his poison far less valuable, if not worthless altogether. A CIA Agent named Nathan Weiss, who was operating under the name of Dean West, and Inspector Mike Riley from the Chicago Police Department had cornered Barclay in a warehouse. He had a hostage, Abbey Short, who was Nathan's girlfriend. Riley had Tyrone Saint John in custody, and had persuaded him to set up a meeting with Barclay at the warehouse, where they planned to arrest him. But Kirkpatrick had followed them there and in the ensuing melee, during which Kirkpatrick killed Saint John and was injured and captured, Barclay managed to escape. Dean and Riley chased him through the streets of Chicago to the offices of Chong Li Enterprises Barclay had arranged to sell the stolen formula for the cancer cure to Chong Li.

Chong Li's son San Li's henchman caught Barclay, tied him to a chair, and believing that

Barclay had murdered his father, San Li burned him badly on the chest with a red hot poker. Dean West and Mike Riley burst in and there was a firefight. Barclay shot San Li, ran out onto the terrace and Dean chased him. Barclay raised his gun to shoot at him but Dean fired first and when his bullet creased Barclay's skull it knocked him unconscious and he toppled backwards over the wall of the terrace. He fell seventy feet into the murky waters of the docks. Even in July the water was still chilly enough to shock him back to full consciousness. Revived, he took a deep breath and held it, staying under the water and out of sight for as long as he could. Despite the pain from the burn and the wound to his head he swam strongly beneath the surface away from the dock wall and came up between two large container ships which were anchored in the harbour while they waited for a berth. He used their enormous steep hulls for cover. The docks were full to capacity, so guessing that they would be staying there until the morning he waited for nightfall. Then he edged away, slowly making his way down river.

He clambered up the bank to the roadside. He saw a truck coming and exaggerated a stumble into the road as if he was going to fall in front of it, causing the truck to screech to a halt. The driver pulled up off the side of the road and jumped out of the truck, but before he could say anything Barclay grabbed hold of the guy and threw him down the bank. As the guy stopped rolling and tried to get back to his feet Barclay was on him. He grabbed his head and twisted it violently. The vertebrae gave a sickening crack and the guy gasped his last breath. Barclay glanced over his shoulder to make sure no-one else had seen and dragged him behind the trees. He quickly rifled through the guy's pockets and fished out a wallet. A few hundred dollars were in the billfold. Nice, that would come in handy because he needed some fresh clothes and the cash in his pocket would be sodden wet. He felt around to his back trouser pocket for his own wallet. Good, it was still there, he hadn't lost it in the water. In it were a few credit cards made out to the false identities he had acquired over the years. In each of those accounts there was several thousand dollars. That was the only decent thing he could say about Kirkpatrick. The man paid well for Barclay's services when he needed something from him that wasn't strictly above board. Plus a few bribes from criminals whose activities he turned a blind eye to top the balances up. Barclay hid the body as well as he could. Then he went back up to the truck and gave a quick look around. Reassuring himself that he hadn't been spotted he jumped in and drove away to look for a motel where he could hide out for a while to gather his thoughts until the dust settled. He found a suitable place a few miles up the road. A seedy establishment where the grimy unshaven owner was only too happy to pocket the cash without asking too many questions. Barclay checked in for three nights using one of his false IDs.

Later that night he drove the truck into some woodland. He took the can of petrol which was conveniently stored in the trunk and poured the whole contents all over the inside of the vehicle. He stepped back a safe distance, tossed a lighted match through the open window and as the truck burst into flames he walked away back towards the motel.

7pm Thursday 14th September 1995. Albuquerque.

Jake Barclay had laid low in New Mexico since his escape from the docks. He used the time to re-energise himself and decide on a course of action. During the whole time his only train of thought in his unhinged mind was one of revenge against everyone who he blamed for what had gone wrong with his plans during the preceding months. Miles Kirkpatrick and Tyrone Saint- Brown were already dead, and he regretted that neither of them had perished by his hand. But he consoled himself in the knowledge that by the time he'd finished the rampage that he was about to embark upon there would still be a hefty body count.

He cleared all the funds out of his accounts, and with a newly shaven head and face went to see one of the few contacts he could still trust, a counterfeiter who conveniently operated in Albuquerque, not too far from where he was hiding out. The guy's name was Lance Cassidy, a middle-aged dwarf who had deformed hands and beady little eyes. How he managed to do such amazing quality work was a miracle, but he could, and he was a master of his craft. He worked out of the back of a gas station which from the front gave the appearance of being an ordinary auto-mechanic's workshop. His little workroom was concealed from the public, and the only people who knew he was there were the owner of the gas station, who was pleased to keep shtum about him and his dubious customers in return for the inflated rent Cassidy paid him.

Barclay first met Cassidy about four years ago when he was working for the CIA and his boss Kirkpatrick believed that he was supplying major criminals with false documentation. He sent Barclay to bring him in. But instead, the two came to an arrangement. Barclay thought that he might need Cassidy's services one day. So, in return for a promise from him of access to whatever he needed, whenever he needed it, he reported back that Cassidy had flown the coup and disappeared. He was smart enough to realise that if he refused then one of two things would happen. Either he would spend a long time behind bars, which was the better of the two, as the alternative was that Barclay would squash him like a bug with his bare hands. Strangely enough Barclay found that he had a soft spot for the little guy. He admired the way he had overcome the shitty disadvantages that life had thrown at him and was making the best of his talents. He couldn't work out why. Maybe it was because he felt an affinity with him. So, whenever he made use of his services, he paid him well.

Barclay had called Cassidy to tell him he would be arriving in half an hour. In anticipation of a decent payday, Cassidy responded with a cheerful 'No problem Jake. I'll have everything ready for you. I'll let the grease-monkeys in the front know.'

Barclay walked through the workshop and rapped on the door at the back. Cassidy saw Barclay's face on the screen he had on his desk and pressed the button to release the door. Barclay strode into the cigarette-smoke filled office and coughed in disgust as he waved his hand up and down in front of his face to clear some of the fumes away. The two men exchanged minimal pleasantries. 'Hell man,'

Barclay said, 'that smoking is going to kill you!'

'Tell me about it,' Cassidy said, with the ever-present smouldering cigarette hanging out of his mouth. Declining to comment on Barclay's changed appearance, he efficiently set about his business. He took new photographs, and two hours later Barclay had purchased two replacement false identities from him, along with passports, and driver's licenses. Cassidy also opened two new accounts for Barclay in local banks and provided him with credit cards. Barclay thanked him, paid him in cash and left. He drove straight into town, hefted a bag which contained the rest of the cash out of the trunk, walked into both banks in turn and using his new false IDs he deposited the money evenly across the two accounts. He also changed both of the pin numbers.

'Just in case.' he thought, 'You can't trust any bastard these days.'

He couldn't bring himself to kill Cassidy. Apart from the fact that he liked him, he had a feeling he was going to need him again.

Now he was back, skulking around the outskirts of Oak Park, a nine-mile drive west out of

Chicago on the Eisenhower Expressway. From his shirt pocket he pulled his newly acquired throw away mobile phone and a tatty business card which he'd carefully dried out after his swim in Lake Michigan. He could just about make out the number. He punched the keys.

Three rings, then, 'Johnson here,' the squeaky voice at the other end answered.

'Johnson, this is Brown,' Barclay said, not giving his real name. 'I left something with you a few months ago for safe keeping. I said I would be back for it. Well I'm here now, and I need it, tonight.'

Johnson, a skinny, bourbon guzzling and insignificant looking little runt of a man felt his guts turn to water as he instantly recognised the voice of the vicious looking man mountain who had barged into his small IT store some months before. Barclay was bleeding from head injuries. Johnson was too petrified to ask how or where he had sustained them.

'Copy these now,' Barclay had said, thrusting some CDs at Johnson. 'Give me back the originals and keep the copies locked up for me. Don't read them, just copy them. Don't tell anyone about it either or I'll come back and separate your skin from your body, little piece by little piece.' He opened his torn jacket to reveal the hilt of a huge hunting knife sticking up from his belt. He had purchased it a few minutes earlier from the camping store along the block. Johnson could also see a revolver nestling in the guy's shoulder holster. 'And don't think I won't find out, because I will. Are you brave enough to take that chance Mister...?'

'Johnson, Pete Johnson, and don't worry sir, I won't even look at them. I'll make the copies in front of you and seal them in an envelope. You can even sign across the seal so you'll know it hasn't been opened. A-a-and I promise you sir, I won't tell a soul.'

'I won't worry. It's you who has to do the worrying.' Jake Barclay stared at him with his deadly cold grey eyes, to make sure that Johnson got the message.

Johnson flinched, then moved quickly and did exactly as he said. He handed the originals back, with a shaking hand. The guy frightened him so much he thought he was going to pee his pants.

'Here sir, it's on the house, and here's my card, just call me when you want the copies and I'll deliver them to you.'

Johnson's generosity went unnoticed. The CDs were snatched without a word and the huge man threw a five-dollar bill down on the counter, turned and strolled from the shop, as calmly as if he had just purchased a Christmas card. Johnson waited just a second to make sure the man wasn't coming back. Then he snatched up the money and rushed to the bathroom, stuck his head down the toilet bowl and deposited the contents of his recently consumed evening meal, which was mostly Wild Turkey, the liquid, not the feathered variety.

That was nearly two months ago. He'd almost begun to believe that he had imagined it in one of his regular drunken stupors. That maybe he wasn't going to hear from him again. No such luck. If it was a nightmare it was recurring. The guy was back, on the phone, sounding just as menacing as he had at that first face to face encounter.

'Of course, of course, when and where would

you like me to bring them to you Mister Brown?'

He listened to the instructions. 'What time sir? Of course, I know the place, I'll see you there.'

He retrieved the package from the small safe in the office at the back of the shop and locking up behind him scurried out of the rear door to his old pick up which he kept parked in the alleyway.

Silently praying that the beaten-up vehicle would start first time, he breathed a foul, bourbon stinking sigh of relief as the tired engine fired on the third attempt. He headed out to the edge of town to meet the monster. In the back of his mind was a nagging feeling that it was going to be his last car ride. If he was honest with himself, he would have said that his life was such a shitty waste of an existence anyway. A nagging wife, mounting debts. Maybe someone was going to do for him what he didn't have the balls to do himself and end it all for him.

He parked his pick-up at the point the man he now knew as Brown had told him.

'Be at the two-mile marker south of town at ten

forty-five tonight' he'd said. 'Leave the pick-up and walk into Columbus Park. Don't worry if you can't see me. I'll be watching to make sure you're alone. I'll come to you. Don't be late.'

Barclay had deliberately said ten forty-five because the park closed at eleven. Not only would there be very few people, if any at all in the park at that time of night, but it would also give him the time to do what he needed to do and be out of the park before it closed.

Johnson walked through the park gates. It was getting darker now. He kept checking behind him after almost every step. He stopped to take another long swig of bourbon. As he put the bottle to his mouth he froze at the chilling sound of Barclay's voice. He quaked as Barclay suddenly stepped out from behind a tree and appeared in front of him. Even with Barclay's newly shaven head and face, the sheer bulk of him meant that he was still instantly recognisable

'Stop there, that'll be fine. Now, where's my package?'

'Here Mister Brown, I have it here, exactly as it was when you left it with me. Look, unopened and still signed across the seal' Johnson held the envelope out, his hand shaking so much that Barclay could hear the CDs rattling around inside it. But Barclay didn't take the envelope. Instead he stepped forward, grabbed Johnson's wrist in his massive left hand and pulled him violently onto the hunting knife, which he had kept concealed in his other hand behind his back. He plunged it up into Johnson's stomach, through his left lung, and with so much force that the tip of the long blade sliced into his heart, killing Johnson so quickly that he didn't even have time to scream. Instead a gurgling sigh escaped from his throat as his last bourbon smelling breath left him, and he crumpled down onto the tarmac of the pathway. The blood seeped from the wound and stained the tarmac as it soaked into it, streaming beneath his body. Barclay knelt, turned Johnson roughly onto his back and retrieved the envelope. 'Thanks Johnson, but I can't leave any loose ends, no witnesses. Especially one who's likely to blab once he's got a few drinks in him.' He easily lifted Johnson's body and tossed it deep into the bushes, guessing that when the warden arrived to lock the park it would be too dark for him to see the blood on the path.

Jake Barclay, the ruthless killing machine was back. He once again had the CDs. On them was the formula for a cure for cancer. It mattered not to him that Lloyd had his originals back and that these were now worthless. So, he wasn't going to try to find another buyer. What would be the point? He had other matters to attend to, some debts of honour to repay, revenge to exact, starting in Washington DC. This was now a matter of personal pride. So, first stop Washington. Then back to Chicago. He made his way back to the stolen black sedan with the number plates he had removed from a matching car. Nobody bothers to report stolen number plates, and the vehicle that they came from won't be reported stolen either, so there was very little chance of his recently acquired ride being detected. Johnson's body wouldn't be discovered until the park reopened at six o'clock in the morning, giving him plenty of time to be on his way out of Chicago.

'I hope you are going to be at home brother,' he muttered to himself as he climbed into the car. 'I'm coming to pay you a visit.'

10.00 Saturday 16th September 1995. Washington.

Nathan Weiss sat across from his wife Abbey in Mo's coffee house, a few minutes' walk from his office in Washington DC. He gazed into her sapphire blue eyes.

By ten o'clock in the morning, apart from a few stragglers, the breakfast crowd had usually dispersed.

'What's wrong Nathan?' Abbey asked anxiously.

He started to speak, but hesitated, worried that he was going to upset her.

'Please,' she said, 'something is worrying you, what is it?'

'I'm not happy Abbey, and I have been meaning to tell you for a few weeks now, but I was concerned about how you would react.'

Her eyes glistened as tears formed. 'Unhappy,' she said, 'but we've only been married for...'

Nathan realised immediately what she was thinking and reached across the table to grasp her hands. 'No, not with you silly, you make me happier than I could ever have imagined. It's work, the office, things are not right.'

'But I thought that with your promotion, when they made you the youngest Assistant Director?'

'That's the problem Abbey. The promotion, it was just PR, on two counts. First, by giving me that promotion, with all the publicity it brought with it they sneakily diverted attention away from the mess that Kirkpatrick had dropped them in. Secondly, it was also supposed to make me feel better after I killed Jake. But I was only a rookie. OK, I had done some field training, but nowhere near as much as most of the other agents. I had even been on a few assignments, but they were reasonably safe. Kirkpatrick was keeping me on ice. Then when the opportunity arose, he brought me in because he wanted me to track down Jake. He'd sussed out that there was history between us. Then, finding out that he was my brother came as a shock to all of us. And it broke my mother's heart. To lose a husband and two children is tough, even if she didn't know one of them. I'm going to have to keep my eye on her.'

He trailed off thinking about his parents, and

how he was supposed to become a lawyer, to fulfill his father's dream. He'd decided he wasn't going to tell his mother that Jake was the baby who she thought had died at a few days old. But the story broke all over the TV and the press, so he'd had no choice. She cried for days. Nathan wasn't sure if she was crying because her son was dead or because of the monster he had become. The violent life, killing at will, including her daughter Leah, his own sister.

But the undeniable truth was that Nathan had enjoyed the adrenalin rush, and the thrill of the catch. And he wasn't going to get that out of sitting behind a lousy desk. He was too young to spend his days like that. He wanted to go out on assignments. But he was worried that if it meant he would be away for any length of time he would be leaving his mother, who visited as often as time and his busy schedule would allow. He also knew that Abbey wanted to start a family. So, he had kept it to himself, until now, when he had asked her to meet him for a coffee so that he could run it by her. The problem was, he didn't have a clue how or where to begin.

But he needn't have worried.

'You want to go back out to it don't you?' she said.

Nathan's jaw dropped and he gazed at Abbey in sheer astonishment.

'Why on earth should I be surprised?' he said.

'That you know me better than I know myself.'

'Yes, I do. And I'm not blind either Nathan. I've sensed it for weeks now. I have been waiting for you to tell me. And I'm ok with it I suppose. But there is one condition.'

'Ok, I'm listening.'

'More coffee guys?' the pretty Mexican waitress said as she breezed up to the table.

'No thanks, we're fine,' they both replied in unison.

'I'm still listening,' Nathan quipped.

'You have to have a partner.'

'Of course.'

'Someone you trust.'

'Of course, again. Where is this leading?'

'And someone I can trust to watch my husband's back.'

'Don't tell me, you want to join the CIA and come out on assignments with me.'

They both laughed.

'Mike Riley.'

Nathan was stunned. 'Mike Riley? He hates the CIA. Most cops do. Anyway, he retired last month. We're going to his retirement party next Thursday, with Lionel and Rebecca, remember? 'Anyway,' Nathan repeated, 'he would never agree to it.'

'Well I think he will, Abbey said. 'If you don't believe me, you can ask him yourself.'

'And when am I supposed to do that?'

Abbey smiled at Nathan with a triumphant look on her face. 'This evening,' she said, 'he's coming for dinner.'

'He's in Washington?'

'I called him yesterday and said that we needed to talk, and not over the telephone. I told him it couldn't wait until next week so he agreed to come up today. He's driving down today, staying with us tonight and driving back tomorrow.'

'Driving, not flying?'

'Well, apparently our brave policeman doesn't like to fly. He prefers to drive.'

Nathan sat back in the chair and stared at his

wife in amazement.

'OK' he said, smiling at his wife, this beautiful woman, who he adored. She had not only seen that he was unhappy, she had taken pre-emptive steps to help him and spoken to Mike Riley. He had trouble believing how lucky he was to have found her again. How close he had twice come to losing her, first to Kirkpatrick, and then to Barclay. But he wasn't going to repay her kindness by being selfish.

He finally spoke, 'OK, OK, just one second,' he said. 'What about our plans to start a family? I don't want you to think I'm asking you to put that on hold.'

Her radiant smile seemed to light up the whole coffee house.

'Well, it's actually a little late for you to worry about that. You see Mister Weiss, you're not the only one with secrets. I have been keeping one of my own.'

For the second time in only a few minutes Nathan's jaw dropped open again. Then his face seemed to fold in half with the broadest of smiles. He jumped up, sending the chair flying. The other patrons stopped in mid-conversation to look across at them to see what the commotion was all about. They relaxed as Nathan took his wife in his arms and kissed her tenderly.

'When did you find out, why didn't you tell me?'

'Yesterday,' she said coyly, and when you suggested we met for a coffee I thought it would be a good opportunity to tell you. But I couldn't tell you I'm having a baby. That wouldn't be exactly true.'

'Why not? What do you mean?' Nathan asked, a worried expression showing on his face.

'Because Nathan, we're having twins!'

'Twins! How long have you known? I mean,' he glanced at her stomach, 'you don't look, ….. how far are you ….. whatever the expression is?' he blustered.

'Three months.'

'Three months? And you haven't told me? Why? I don't get it.'

'I couldn't say anything because I wasn't sure, and I didn't want to disappoint you in case I was wrong. Even the doctor wasn't certain. Things were, you know, happening that one wouldn't expect. And then the doctor told me today it wasn't only definite, but it's going to be twins.' Her smile lit up her whole face and Nathan fell in love with her all over again.

He hugged her again. 'Then shouldn't I be getting you home so that you can put your feet up?'

As he spoke a cold shiver ran down his spine. He turned sharply and looked around the coffee house.

'What's the matter, Nathan, what's wrong?'

Over the months that had passed, Nathan had been mulling over the chain of terrible events which led up to Kirkpatrick's capture and Barclay's death. He had realised recently he hadn't felt that awful shiver down his spine for a while. His analytical brain examined all of the situations when he had experienced it previously and he realised with some dread that it had always been when Barclay was close by. The last time he felt it was at Kirkpatrick's funeral, and although he couldn't see Barclay, he sensed his presence. He had dismissed it, telling himself he must be wrong, that Jake Barclay was gone. He was dead. And If Nathan's bullet hadn't killed him then he had surely drowned in the depths of the freezing water at the Chicago docks.

Or had he?

The shiver ran from his neck to his lower back, as if someone had stepped on his grave, and then it was gone.

'Nothing sweetheart', he said, turning around and quickly sweeping the coffee house with his eyes. He turned back to her and smiled. 'It's a bit chilly in here don't you think?'

Jake Barclay sat across the road in his navy sedan and watched the café. Being impetuous had cost him dearly so he was going to take his time. He decided to keep an eye on Nathan for a few days, to track his movements. He would be happy just killing him, but if his wife was there as well then all well and good. The way Barclay saw it, Abbey was also partly responsible for everything going wrong, so if she got in the way, then that was her look out.

07.00 Friday 15th September 1995. Oak Park.

Sheriff Hal Mulhans was in seventh heaven. He

had just run 80 yards to score the winning touchdown in the Rose Bowl. Two giant quarterbacks had hoisted him onto their shoulders and they were parading him around the ground. The crowd were deliriously shouting his name. 'Mulhans, Mulhans', they called as he waved to them, acknowledging their adoration. The quarterbacks put him down and he fell into the arms of two gorgeous blonde cheerleaders, pawing their backsides and ecstatically groping them all over their young firm bodies while they giggled in encouragement. 'Mulhans, Mulhans', the crowd continued to bray, but then the voices from the stands seemed to fade to just one solitary caller, accompanied by a loud persistent banging. The Rose Bowl faded as he opened his eyes. 'Sheriff Mulhans,' the banging continued, but it was coming from his front door. He struggled out of bed, mourning the dream he had just lost and shaking his head awake and back to reality.

'I'm coming, hold your darn horses and stop that banging" he shouted, flinging the door open.

Deputy Jorgens was standing there, and at the sight of Mulhans's naked body, with his flabby white belly hanging down to almost his knees, he averted his eyes and instead focused on the floor.

'What's the matter Jorgens, ain't you never seen a naked man before?'

'We gotta problem sheriff,' the deputy said, ignoring the question.

'Well son, it had better be a good one,' Mulhans said looking at his watch, 'because it's seven o'clock in the fucking morning and you just woke me up from the dream of dreams. Two blondes, not one but two, there for the taking, I didn't know which one to have first, and you're standing here telling me you gotta problem. Sonny, your problem had better be as good as mine or I'm gonna kick your skinny ass around the block, that's for damn sure.

'It's Pete Johnson sheriff. Art Clancey was out on his early morning run through the park when the warden found him.'

'What drunk again? Well tell him to dump Clancey back home to sleep it off. Why in blazes is that my problem? If that's all you woke me up for, after I've finished kicking you round the block, I'm going to rip that fuckin' badge off your chest and ram it where the sun don't shine. Why you bringin' these problems to me? I don't need this job anyway. I don't even want to be here no more.'

'No, sheriff, he wasn't drunk, well he might have been, but he's sure as hell dead now. Stabbed, well that's what Art said the warden told him. Looks like he's been there all night. Coyotes had already been at him. The body was in a bit of a mess.'

Mulhans stopped ranting. 'Now boy, you're right. That there is a problem. This here is a nice quiet town. We ain't got no murderers here. We just got normal gentle folk. It must be someone from outa town. Why would anyone here want to kill Pete Johnson? He was a piss-head I grant you, and as crooked as a witch's grin, but he was harmless enough. OK, wait while I get dressed, then you'd better take me to the crime-scene.'

19.30 Saturday 16th September 1995. Washington.

Mike Riley approached The Weiss's front door. He paused a moment before ringing the bell. His thoughts wandered to thirty five years ago..

As usual the door to his parents' house was open so he walked straight in. The house was alive with people buzzing around, family and close friends.
'Hey,' somebody shouted, 'the birthday boy is here.'
A raucous chorus of Happy Birthday went up, 'Happy birthday dear Michael, happy birthday to you.'
He'd suspected for a few days that his parents were up to something so he feigned surprise as smiling broadly he walked around the ground floor of the house, going from room to room, shaking hands, kissing cheeks, finally ending up in the kitchen, where he embraced his parents.
'Thanks mum, dad, lovely party, I wasn't expecting it.'
'Like hell you weren't,' his father said, 'you didn't think we would put on a spread for your

twenty first birthday? Where did you think I've been going all those hours when I've left you on your own at the bar? Good practice for when you take over when I retire in a few years eh?'

Michael didn't respond. He just looked at his father with a pained expression on his face.

'What's up son, what's that strange look for?'

'Nothing dad, talk in the morning eh?'

'No Mike, we'll talk now, what the hell is the problem?'

'Pat, leave the boy alone, it's his birthday,' his mother intervened.

'Mary, please stay out of it, Mike, what's got into you?' Pat Riley's voice was rising as his Irish temper started to get the better of him. People turned in surprise to look at the developing row that was suddenly turning the party into a potential brawl.

'Not now, please dad, leave it alone, we'll talk later, I promise.' Before Pat could say anything Mike leaned forward and hugged him again, and went to join his friends in the other room, leaving his father staring into an empty space. Pat made to follow him, but his wife stepped in front of him. 'Please Pat,' she begged, 'leave him for now, there'll be plenty of time after everybody has left.' Pat sighed heavily and backed down. 'Ok' he said, 'we'll leave it for now, but I want it sorted tonight. I want to know what the hell has got into that kid.'

Three hours later when all the guests had left the three of them sat around the kitchen table with a mug of coffee.

'What's going on son?' Pat asked.

Michael stared at his father trying to find the words. 'Pop, I don't want to take over the bar. I want to be a cop.'

'A cop, are you crazy, a cop in New York. Do you know how dangerous that is?'

Mike didn't answer. He was shocked by his father's response, because he had been a cop himself before he had retired and bought the bar.

Pat Riley stared at his son, as if agonising over what to say.

'Look son, I know I was a cop, and I'm proud of you for wanting to join the force as well, and I'm sure your mother is too.'

His mother nodded in agreement, but knew it was best to remain silent.

'But it's so different now,' his father continued, 'things have totally changed, and not for the better either.'

'How?'

'The fact that I was a cop means nothing any more, not to the guys I have to pay protection money to, if anything its costs me more.'

'Protection money, what the hell are you talking about'?

'I try to keep you out of it Mike. I make sure you're not there when they come for their cut. The fact is once they find out my son is a cop, I don't know what they will do. Mike, they might not take the news well. They will assume you know I'm paying them off and might worry what you will do about it. They might even come after you to stop you making trouble for them.' His father put his head in his hands, ashamed that he had been forced to admit to his son that he, an ex-cop, was now paying the mob for his existence.

'What do you want me to do pop?' Mike said, trying to hide the shock.

'Look son, I don't want to stop you being a cop if that's what you really want to do. Just not here in New York. Move away, America ain't such a big place anymore. You can fly anywhere in a few hours these days. But once you decide where to go, for your own safety you mustn't come back here. We'll come to visit you, I promise.'

'What about the bar? You said you want to retire in the next few years? And will you be OK? How long have you been paying those guys anyway? I had no idea.'

'Don't worry about that son. In a funny sort of way you going will help me to make my mind up. With you gone I might as well retire now and enjoy the rest of my life in peace. If there is such a thing as peace living with your mother.'

They all laughed as his mother playfully elbowed him in the ribs.

Pat became serious again. 'Son, there are plenty of cops coming up for retirement pretty soon who will be looking for bars to buy. So I'll sell it easily enough. And as long as I carry on paying these guys on time until I do, they'll leave me alone. They're sensible enough not to make the payments too steep. There's no point in them crippling me is there? I'd only have to shut the *place down and then they'd get nothing. And I'll tell whoever's buying it what's going on, then they can decide if they want to get involved or not. I'm sure it won't come as a surprise to them and I wouldn't want to keep it from them anyway. Their finding out afterwards could cause me a bigger problem.'*

Mike looked at his mother and could see from her sad expression that the protection payments were not news to her.

'Are you sure pop? I hate to let you down. I could stay if you want me to but I do want to do this?'

'Look son, it was my dream for you to take over, but I don't want to stand in the way of your dreams either.'

'OK,' Mike said. 'Where do you suggest I go then?'

Pat thought for a minute, then he smiled and clicked his fingers. 'Chicago, yeah, there's loads of Irish folk there. You'll fit in well, and I still know a few of the boys in the force there. They'll make you feel welcome and help you settle in. Just you make sure that you graduate from that academy with flying colours. And son, I want you to make me one promise.'

'Sure, what's that pop?'

'That when you become a high flying cop you don't think that you can come back here like Elliot Ness and take on the mob. Leave it to the FBI, whose job it is. And anyway I'll be long gone from the bar by then.'

'It's a deal pop,' Mike said.

The two men stood up and embraced, then his mother, with tears streaming down her face stood and joined in the family huddle.

They all raised their coffee cups, 'To Chicago!' they said in unison.

Mike Riley's thoughts returned to the present day and he rang the bell. As he pushed it he heard the musical chimes and waited for the door to open.

Nathan stepped out and extended his hand. 'Hi Mike,' he said.

'Hi, who are you tonight,' Dean, Nathan or The Scarlet Pimpernel?'

Nathan smiled at the policeman he had turned to for help just a few months ago. The man who was now his friend.

'Nathan will do nicely thanks, come inside Mike, Abbey is waiting.'

Nathan felt the familiar chill down his back, which he knew wasn't from the weather. Before closing the door he looked tentatively up and down the street. Seeing nothing, he shook his head and shut the door.

They walked through the hallway together, to the kitchen where Abbey stood, wearing a bright blue apron, which enhanced the sapphire blue of her eyes. She was busy stirring a saucepan of soup. She turned to greet them.

'Hello Mike,' she trilled. 'Lovely of you to come.
'

'Well,' he said, 'apart from wanting to see how your old man was getting on, I gotta say I was intrigued by your sudden invitation. I tried to work out what it could be about on the long drive down.'

'Why'd you drive Mike?' Nathan said. 'You never told me you were scared of flying.'

'What? No, don't be daft. Of course I'm not, I just prefer the independence of the road, that's all. I can stop when I like, for something to eat, or drink. Talking of drinking, this is a dry old ship by the way.'

'What, oh sorry Mike, I'm forgetting my manners, what would you like to drink?'

'Thought you'd never ask, bourbon, on the rocks please.'

'No problem, follow me.'

'They moved into the lounge. 'Have a seat Mike,' Nathan said as he went over to the drinks cabinet to prepare their drinks. He handed Mike the glass.

'So Nathan, how is it going?' Mike studied Nathan, waiting for an answer.

'It's been tough Mike,' Nathan said. 'I know we were only working together for a few days, everything seemed to happen very quickly, but I miss it.'

'Miss what?'

'You know, the adrenalin rush, the camaraderie.'

Mike looked at Nathan in surprise. 'Really?' he said. 'Funny, I never took you for being crazy.'

An unnerving cold feeling crept down Nathan's back again, which made him shudder and prompted him to quietly say, 'Well if you think that's crazy, wait till you hear what else I've got to tell you.'

Mike noticed Nathan was suddenly looking a little uneasy.

'Are you OK kid?'

'Sure, just a bit cold that's all.'

'Go on then, I'm listening.'

Nathan checked to make sure that Abbey was out of earshot. 'I don't think Jake Barclay is dead.'

Riley's jaw dropped open. 'What the hell are you talking about Nathan? I saw the whole thing, you shot him, and he went over the wall into Lake Michigan. They never found him, I'll grant you, but if your bullet didn't kill him, then he must have drowned. His body probably drifted out to the Chicago River. He's either laying on the riverbed or he's fed an awful lot of fish. A damn good job if you ask me. I mean, I'm sorry, I know he turned out to be your brother and all that, but he was a vicious prick.'

'I'm not so sure anymore that he's dead Mike,' Nathan said. 'I'm just not so sure. It's difficult to explain, but I can sense he's close.'

Mike's eyebrows rose a notch, but before he could say anything else Abbey called to them.

'Dinner's ready, come and sit down guys.'

'Please Mike, don't say anything to Abbey about this.'

'Ok,' Mike said. 'But you and I will need to talk this through.'

'Sure, don't worry. When Abbey has told you why she asked you here tonight we'll get plenty of opportunity.'

'OK, now I'm intrigued.'

They obediently went to the kitchen and sat down at the table where a smiling Abbey placed a bowl of steaming freshly made soup in front of each of them.

Outside, just along from the house Jake Barclay sat grinning in his car. He couldn't believe his luck. Mike Riley, the cop who had been instrumental in scuppering his plans months before, was only in the Weiss's house. All three of them, together, like pigs in a poke. What a brilliant stroke of luck. 'I'll pick Riley off when he comes back out, then go in and take care of the two of them.'

16.00 Tuesday 22nd August 1995. New York.

Krystal Brown, the head of The New York Port Authority sat behind her huge oak desk in her office in the World Trade Centre. She was stunning looking, and slim. She stood at five foot nine in her bare feet, and had long straightened raven black hair and sparkling brown eyes. She was only in her mid-thirties, but she was already on her third husband. She had thoughtfully chosen, targeted and won each of them. She had even more thoughtfully removed the first two. Her third, a flashy Greek property magnate in his mid-fifties, was on the way out as well. He just didn't know it yet. He had no other family, and now that he had bequeathed his two hundred and fifty million dollar fortune solely to her, together with his twenty or so properties in countries spread all around the globe, Aristos Mecadenos had unwittingly become a work in progress. Through all of her marriages she had insisted on retaining her maiden name, having long ago dropped the 'Saint' in an effort to avoid linking her name with that of her three younger brothers, Tyrone, Earl and Jethro Saint-Brown, who were always in one kind of trouble or another.

Her office was like her home, fitted with the finest furnishings and adorned with luxury accoutrements. She considered that she had earned her lofty status, having grafted her fingers to the bone since her early teens to achieve it. If she wanted to surround herself with the products of her success, nobody was going to deny her the right to do so.

She had reached her elevated position by using her wits, and when she needed to, by calling upon the brawn of her brothers, who were also her enforcers. She controlled pretty much everything that went in or out of several United States harbours, making sure that she received her cut on every consignment. Without her say so, goods would either lay going rotten or gathering dust in the ships' holds while they were waiting to be offloaded, or in the warehouses waiting to be despatched. Very often the ships carried freight that was not logged on the cargo manifest, and if the ships' captains didn't want to cooperate and allow it to be loaded, they would experience extremely unpleasant and painful visitations from her brothers until they saw the light and complied.

Earl and Jethro sat listening to her intently. Tyrone was absent, killed in a shoot-out at a warehouse at the Chicago docks some six weeks ago. This was the first time the three had met since Tyrone's death, her two other brothers having spent four weeks in a New Jersey State prison awaiting trial for burglary. She had managed to grease the appropriate palms to put frighteners in the right places in order to secure their release last week. Now they sat together in her office trying to piece together the circumstances leading up to his death.

'So, let's go over it again, when did you last hear from Tyrone Krys?' Earl, the oldest brother asked. He was only marginally taller than Tyrone, almost identical facially and in stature, the two of them quite often having being mistaken for twins. But he was placid and even tempered. Even though he had no problem using violence to make his point, he was way behind Tyrone in the meanness stakes.

Jethro however, the youngest sibling, was the runt of the litter. He was five foot six tall and skinny built, without an ounce of muscle. He irritatingly and permanently whinged in a high pitched squeaky voice. But he was a really nasty piece of work. He made Tyrone and Earl look like pussy cats in comparison. He always carried a selection of blades with him, and would look for the slightest excuse to carve someone into little pieces, regardless of their gender. Over the years he had been questioned several times about random murders, most of the victims having been hookers. It was only due to Krystal's influence and her far reaching tentacles that the police enquiries had gone no further.

'I've told you a hundred times,' Krystal shouted, 'he used to call me nearly every other day, so that I knew where he was and what he was up to. Two reasons. First, in case I needed him back here and second in case he'd got himself into trouble. So I would always know where he was.'

'Yeah, we got that sis,' Earl said, but when was the last time?'

'I lost touch with him the first week in July. He was in Chicago. Kirkpatrick had him tailing some rookie CIA guy that he'd sent there to make some people disappear. But he told Tyrone that he didn't trust the rookie to do it. I already told you that. Then, it all got very complicated, first Jake Barclay showed up, then Kirkpatrick himself. Tyrone said it was like some comedy act out of a slapstick movie, everybody chasing everybody else. Then a lot of shit hit some very big fans, blew a lot of crap all over the place. Shooting in the street, car chases the works. Tyrone told me that he'd arranged to meet Barclay, but I never heard from him again, till I got word through one of my cop contacts that he was dead. Because of Kirkpatrick's involvement a lot of the details were hushed up. So I don't know who killed him.'

'My money is on Barclay,' Jethro ventured.

'And mine.' Earl said. 'So what are we going to do about it?'

'I agree.' said Krystal. 'So, you two are going to find Barclay. And when you do you are going bring him to me so that I can peel the skin off him, nice and slow.'

Jethro's mouth spread in a shining white toothy grin at the thought.

'No need for you to trouble. I'll do that Krys,' he said.

'No, you won't Jethro,' she said, glaring at him angrily. 'You'll do exactly as I fucking said and bring him here, to me.'

Jethro was about to argue, but seeing Krystal's face he kept quiet and went into a sulk instead.

'He's dead though ain't he?' Earl ventured.

Krystal cut in, her voice chilling and toneless.

'That's what they've said. But they never found his body, and from what Tyrone told me, Barclay don't die that easy. So, he ain't dead unless I see his fucking lifeless body either on a slab in a morgue or in the ground. Get your asses out of here, both of you. See what you can find out. And this time stay the fuck out of trouble. I can't bail either of you out again. Start in Chicago, that's where he was last seen at. I'll call Sergeant Donaghy and set up a meet for you. You remember him?'

'Yeah, I remember him,' whined Jethro. 'You sent us down there last year to give him a pay-off. He counted the money right in front of me.

He gave me a cross-eyed look like it wasn't enough. The fat Irish fuck was lucky I didn't cut his damned ears off. I wanted to, but lucky for him Earl and Tyrone stopped me.'

Krystal ignored her brother. Instead of replying she stood up and peered at the two of them over her desk. 'Well what the hell are you both still sitting there for?' she screamed. 'Get going, and call me when you get there.'

The two men, who if anybody else had spoken to them like that, would have torn his, or for that matter her head off, quaked under the angry gaze of their sister. They both jumped out of their seats and like two chastened naughty little schoolboys they scampered towards the door of her office.

'One more thing,' she called out as they were about to swing it open. They stopped to look back at her.

'Don't go doing anything crazy. Especially you Jethro. Keep those fucking knives in your belt. Are you hearing me?'

'Sure sis, sure thing, I promise.' The pair of them skulked out.

20.15 Saturday 16th September 1995. Washington.

'That was delicious, thank you Abbey,' Mike Riley said to her as she collected the dinner plates. 'So, tell me, what's on your mind that's so urgent I had to drive here today.'

Abbey glanced mischievously at Nathan.

'Nathan has something he wants to tell you.'

'Me? Why me? it's your idea,' he laughed.

Mike intervened. 'Listen guys, as much as I'm enjoying the banter, will one of you get to the point, please.'

Abbey spoke first. 'Nathan wants to get out from behind his desk and go back out on assignments. He misses that part of the job.'

'Really?' said Mike. 'And you're OK with that? You've only recently got married.'

'I am,' Abbey said. 'But I've made a condition.'

'That he comes back in one piece? That's fair enough I suppose.' Mike wisecracked.

'Not exactly. Abbey means more that we both come back in one piece,' said Nathan, pointing at Mike, then back at himself while throwing a quick smirk at Abbey.

'What do you mean *both*?' Mike spluttered. 'Surely you're not suggesting….'

'I'm not suggesting anything Mike. Abbey is.'

Completely stunned, Mike Riley stared at Abbey across the table. 'Abbey, I'm flattered, really I am. But I've given thirty-five years to law enforcement, and I promised Rita and the kids that I was jacking it in while I still can. Before some lunatic puts a hole in me. Every day it's getting more and more dangerous out there. It's time now. Look, my retirement party is next week. When its finished I intend walking out of that bar, shaking hands with all of the guys, saying "*sayonara*" to them and that will be that. I've bought a nice cabin out by the lake so I'm going to take my boys out there and do some fishing. It's a darn site safer. So, I'm sorry to disappoint you Abbey, it was a nice try, and I don't blame you at all, but it's no dice. Nathan old son, no disrespect to you, but you'll have to find another old putz to nursemaid you.'

Abbey looked at Nathan, her disappointment etched on her face.

'Do you want me to drive home now Abbey, or

am I still OK to finish dinner and spend the night?' Riley kidded, suddenly concerned that he might have upset his hosts.

'Of course not Mike,' Abbey quickly said, 'I suppose it's what I expected you to say really. I'm just concerned about Nathan putting himself in danger again,' she said glancing across at him, 'especially as we are soon going to have extra mouths to feed.'

When the penny dropped, a huge grin spread across Mikes face from ear to ear.

'Jeez, that's amazing. You guys sure didn't hang about did you? Hang on, did you say extra mouths, how many, two three four?'

Nathan laughed while Abbey blushed. 'Two actually, that's enough for starters I think,' she said.

'Aw, that's wonderful,' Mike said. 'As I think you guys would say, *Mazeltov*, I'm delighted for both of you.'

'Thanks Mike,' Abbey said.

'Yeah, thanks Mike,' Nathan echoed.

'So,' Mike said, with an impish smile, 'How was my friend Any Patsprick's funeral? I hear you guys went. That was good of you both.'

Abbey gasped and put her hand to her mouth, unsuccessfully stifling a giggle.

'Any Patsprick was Mike's nickname for Kirkpatrick,' Nathan explained.

'So I guessed,' she said, still giggling.

'We were virtually the only people there,' Nathan said. The subject of the funeral reminded him of the conversation he was having with Mike before dinner.

'Fancy another drink in the garden Mike?' he asked him.

'Go on you two, go and catch up,' Abbey said. 'I'll do the dishes and join you when I'm done.'

'Thanks Abbey,' said Nathan. He went over to the Welsh dresser to pick up a bottle of Jack Daniels and two glasses and made his way outside. Mike followed him out. They sat on the patio at the green wrought iron bistro table with four matching chairs.

'I'm sure Jake's alive,' said Nathan, looking intently at Mike.

'Earlier you only thought, now you are sure. What the hell is going on with you Nathan? You've always struck me as being very level-headed. This isn't like you at all.'

'I'm trying to stay level-headed Mike, but do you recall how I used to feel a cold shiver when I thought he was around, and then out of nowhere he'd suddenly show up and prove me right?'

'Yeah, now you come to mention it. To be truthful I never took a lot of notice. Are you sure it wasn't just a coincidence?'

'Yes Mike, I'm sure. And then, I felt it at Kirkpatrick's funeral. It was as if his eyes were on us. The cold shiver went right down my spine. I tried not to let Abbey see, but it frightened the hell out of me. I've only ever felt it when he was close by. It's spooky, almost as if Leah is warning me. And then, twice today, this morning when I was having a coffee in town with Abbey, and then just after you arrived tonight. I'm telling you Mike, the bastard is alive, and he's here, in DC. I think he's targeting us, that he's after his revenge. Don't forget, we screwed up his plans. And remember his pal the Captain, Mitchell Clark or Clark Mitchell whatever his real name was? He died in the car crash when they were getting away from the Chicago Cancer Clinic with the formula. We both know that was Kirkpatrick's doing, but in Jake's warped mind he probably blames me for that as well.'

'Not just you Nathan, I was also responsible. And if you're right, and I'm not saying that you are, but if you are, then he's going to go after both of us.'

'Trust me on this Mike,' Nathan said earnestly, 'I'm right.'

Mike looked in Nathan's eyes. He'd already learned to trust the younger man's instincts.

'Wow', he said, 'OK, let me make a few calls.'

As he pulled his cell phone from his pocket Abbey came out to join them, so he went to the other end of the garden for some privacy.

'What's going on?' she asked.

Nathan looked at her sheepishly.

'Something's come up,' he said, trying to avoid eye contact with her.

Assuming that Mike was dealing with some of his unfinished police business, Abbey didn't press the issue. She sat down at the table next to Nathan, placing the glass of club soda she had brought out of the house down in front of her. Mike ended his call and came back to join them, and unnoticed by Abbey he shot a quick look across to Nathan and nodded. Nathan had a pretty good idea what Mike had arranged on his telephone call and nodded back. The three of them sipped at their drinks as the garden lights cast eerie shadows in the darkness. A light breeze whispered to them as it gently blew through the trees.

By now it was coming up to half past ten. Outside, Barclay was sitting in his car a few doors away from the house, over the road, a little up from the corner of a side-straat, where he could just about see the front of the house. He was becoming increasingly impatient.

'What's Riley doing in there for over two fucking hours?' he ranted. Then the penny dropped. 'The bastard must be staying the night, otherwise he would have come out by now.' He set the alarm on his watch for five the next morning. He would keep watch till the early hours of the morning, then try to catch a few hours' sleep. He stepped out of the car to get some fresh air to help him stay alert for another few hours, crouching low just in case anyone came out. As he exited the car he saw two police cruisers pull up outside the Weiss's house. An officer alighted from one of the vehicles and approached the front door, ambling in the way that only cops do. The cop pushed the doorbell.

Alarmed, Barclay crept back into his car.

'What the hell?' he cursed.

He lay down sideways keeping himself out of sight, lifting his head just enough to peer over the dashboard and keep watch.

Out in the garden they all heard the doorbell. Before Nathan could react Abbey jumped to her feet.

Clearly startled she said, 'who can that be at this hour?' Nathan glanced at Mike and the two men followed her as she quickly walked into the kitchen where she looked at the screen of the video entry-phone system. She could clearly see the police officer and the cruisers outside.

'Nathan,' she said, in a frightened voice, 'why is there a policeman at our front door?'

'I'll deal with him Nathan,' Mike said. 'I suggest you explain to Abbey.'

'Please Nathan,' pleaded Abbey, 'tell me what's going on. Why is there a policeman here?'

'Mike asked him to come.'

'Whatever for?'

'I think Jake Barclay is around. I can sense that he's here Abbey, and I'm worried. I told Mike and he called the local guys to get us some protection. That isn't the sort of thing that I was trained for.'

'Why do you think he's here? I thought you said he was dead. Did you lie to me Nathan?'

'Of course not Abbey, I give you my word. I would never do that,' he said pulling her close to him. 'Let Mike deal with the police and I'll explain it to you afterwards, I promise.'

'OK.' Said Abbey softly. They hugged each other and from behind the kitchen door they watched Mike as he spoke to the policeman.

From over the road Barclay saw Mike Riley answer the door and start speaking with the cop. He watched as Mike gesticulated, sweeping his arm around and indicating in various directions. Mike's eyes settled on Barclay's car, just distinguishable by the glow of a nearby street-light. He pointed to it.

The cop stared across the road and got back in his car to use his radio. As Barclay watched he assumed it was to check on the licence plate. The cop got back out of the car, holding a torch. His partner got out from the other side. They went back to speak with Mike. The three of them were staring.

'Fuck it, muttered Barclay, I don't know how, but I'm blown.'

He threw himself upright, started the car, and so as not to arouse suspicion, reversed slowly back up the side road, swept the car around in a quick three pointer, gunned the engine and drove away in the opposite direction.

8pm Thursday 24th August 1995. A Warehouse at Chicago Docks.

Donaghy didn't like the three Saint-Brown brothers, or their sister for that matter. He was one of the very few people within Krystal's felonious network who was aware that the four were siblings. He knew better than to disclose that information to anybody outside that nefarious circle. He felt sick to his stomach when he thought back to the meeting he had with them last year, when Jethro had one knife at his jugular, and another under his ear lobe. He remembered staring into the boy's dead eyes. They were like patches of the blackest ice. In all of his years in the force he had never been more frightened for his life, or come closer to soiling his pants.

This time they were meeting in a disused section of the docks, behind some old derelict warehouses, which had been left neglected and empty since the occupants had vacated some four years ago and relocated to newly built premises a little further away from the waterfront. The area was now deserted. They were standing fifty yards from the Saint Browns Chevrolet, on the cracked and weed infested access road. A light summer drizzle fell.

And for Donaghy, as Jethro again held the two knives, exactly as he had at that previous meeting, it was deja-vu. The area was deserted. If the brothers decided to kill him here, no-one would be coming to save him.

Earl roughly shoved a small colour picture of Barclay under Donaghy's nose.

'You know him?' he asked.

'Of course I know him. He was involved in a shoot-out a few months back. He drowned in the docks. Why are you looking for a dead man?'

'We know all about the shoot-out. It cost our brother Tyrone his life. But nobody found this guy's body did they? So how do we know he's dead?'

Donaghy guffawed, 'Don't you guys know what the chances are of finding a body once it's gone into those docks? They're practically zero.' But his laugh stuck in his throat when he saw the scowl on Earl's face.

'Well as far as we're concerned,' Earl growled,

'if there ain't no corpse, then he ain't dead. Our sister wants you to find out what you can. Ask around, see if anyone has heard or seen anything from him.'

'Why are you so interested?' Donaghy asked.

Jethro violently jerked his head forward so close to Donaghy's that the two men's noses were almost touching. When Jethro spat out his answer Donaghy instantly regretted his own stupidity at having asked the question. The coldness of Jethro's reply sent shivers down his spine. He wanted to turn his face to the side to avoid the younger man's rank smelling breath, but he daren't in case the blade slit his throat. He couldn't shift his eyes away from Jethro's fixating stare.

'Because we think he killed Tyrone. We're going to find out if he's still alive, and if he is, when we get our hands on him we'll enjoy killing him so slowly that he'll beg us to bring an end to it. Trust me, he'll be wishing that he had fucking drowned.'

Donaghy gulped, and when he did his Adam's apple pushed against the blade, nicking the surface skin. Warm blood pulsed to the surface and trickled down his neck and made its way slowly to inside his shirt. But Jethro hadn't finished yet.

'And anybody who doesn't help us or gets in our way will suffer just as bad. You got that Donaghy?'

Donaghy would have nodded but Jethro's knife was still against his throat. He felt the content of his stomach turning to water and clenched his buttocks together as firmly as he could to avoid embarrassing himself. Even so he couldn't avoid the high pitched squeak emanating from the area of his backside as he broke wind. Jethro smirked wickedly.

'You're looking for the wrong man.' Donaghy said quietly, 'I'm telling you Barclay's dead, and he didn't kill your brother.'

'What? How do you know that?' Earl said. 'Who did?'

'It was the talk of the station. The CIA guy, Kirkpatrick did. He got collared and he was locked away. He died in prison a few weeks later.'

'If that's true why wasn't it in the papers or on the TV?' Jethro sneered.

'I guess because they wanted to keep it quiet and not embarrass the CIA. We were all told to keep our mouths shut or risk being drummed out of the force.'

'I'm not so sure I believe that. Do you know any of the cops who were at the warehouse when Tyrone was killed?' Earl asked him.

'Only Inspector Riley', Donaghy said. 'He headed up the bust.'

'OK,' Earl said. 'Where will I find him?'

'You won't.'

'What the fuck do you mean I won't. Why the hell won't I?'

'Cos he retired. He's quit working.'

'Shit,' Earl shouted. 'Where does he live, this Inspector Riley?'

'I don't know, I swear, I hardly know the guy. But his retirement party is next month. Round about the third week in September. It's open house in a bar downtown. Hang on, I've got it written down.'

The two brothers looked at each other. In unison they frowned and hiked up their eyebrows while they waited for him to fish his notebook out of his shirt pocket. He moved very slowly because Jethro still held the blades up against his throat and ear.

'Here it is,' he said, the relief visible on his fat pink face. 'Thursday, night, September 21st, O'Halloran's bar. It's downtown on South Canal Street.' He tried to smile, but the muscles in his face wouldn't work.

'Don't worry pig, we'll find it. Can I kill him now?' Jethro asked Earl, looking pleadingly across at him.

'No Jethro, you can't.'

'Aw go on bruv', Jethro implored, increasing the pressure beneath Donaghy's ear lobe.'

Donaghy yelped as the sharp blade pierced his skin again and more blood dripped onto his shirt collar.

'No Jethro,' Earl snapped. 'Krystal is pissed enough with us already. Leave it now. Let's go.'

Jethro looked at Donaghy, grinning wickedly, his dark eyes reduced to slits.

'Heck Donaghy, I was only joshing with you man. Gotta go now, see you at the party.'

He withdrew the knives, flicked Donaghy a contemptuous wave and stepped away from him. Like an old time western gunfighter holstering his six-shooters, he stuck the knives back into the sheaths on his belt. Laughing like a demented hyena he loped off behind Earl back towards their Chevy.

Donaghy ran into the nearest deserted warehouse, where thankfully the door was hanging open off the broken hinges. He just made it to the cloakroom in time. Breathing heavily, he ignored the filth and the stench as he quickly undid his belt, dropped his pants to around his ankles, collapsed onto the seat and gratefully released his bowels.

Once he'd finished and cleaned himself he sat there for a few more minutes thinking what to do. Giving the Saint-Browns information was one thing. But knowing that they were intending to create carnage and not doing anything about it was another. He stood up, hitched up his trousers, and to escape the stench shuffled back out into the fresh air. He pulled out his mobile phone and flipped it open and searched for a name. He pressed a saved speed dial number. A hand clamped over his mouth. Cold lips pressed against his ear and as the razor sharp blade of the knife sliced across his throat, the last thing Donaghy heard as he slumped to the ground was Jethro saying, 'Earl changed his mind. We got what we need from you. Krystal will be pissed, but we'll handle that.' Jethro looked around for something to weigh the body down. He found an old truck wheel in the bushes and some rope in the warehouse. Looping the rope through the centre of the wheel he tied it around Donaghy's ankles. He rolled the body along to the edge of the pier and let it drop into the water. He hefted the wheel in after it and Donaghy sank down into the gloomy depths. The phone had slid across the ground and nestled in some nearby weeds. Jethro walked over to it, bent down and picked it up. He took out the sim-card, snapped that and the phone in half, stepped back across and threw it all into the water. Satisfied with his evening's work Jethro grinned from ear to ear and trotted off to re-join Earl. What he hadn't heard when he was disposing of Donaghy's body was Riley saying into the phone 'What's up Donaghy? Speak to me man!' Jethro didn't hear because before he went back to pick up the phone, when Donaghy didn't answer, Riley had assumed it was a pocket call and already disconnected.

9pm Thursday 24th August 1995. New York.

Being a workaholic Krystal was still at her desk. She snatched up the phone when it rang.

'Hi sis, you OK?' the high pitched voice of her brother Jethro whined down the phone. As much as she wanted to know what he and Earl had discovered, she didn't welcome his whinging at her after a long hard day's work.

She got straight to the point. 'What have you found out?'

'Donaghy said that Barclay didn't kill Tyrone. Kirkpatrick did.'

'And you believe him.' Krystal asked.

'Yeah, sure we did. He was too fuckin' scared not to tell us the truth.'

'Well I'm not so sure. I wanna know more, like about how it went down. I'm gonna call him myself and speak to him.'

There was silence on the line. Jethro wasn't expecting this response. His throat suddenly went dry and he croaked through an even higher pitched whinge.

'You can't do that Krystal.'

'What do you mean I can't?' she snapped.

Jethro didn't answer.

'Jethro,' she screamed. 'Answer me, now!'

'Cos he's dead, that's why. He drew his gun on me Krystal. It was me or him, I swear. Ask Earl. He's right here.' Without waiting for her to answer he handed Earl the phone.'

Krystal was relieved to hear Earl's deeper voice, but she was still fuming.

'What the fuck happened Earl? Didn't you hear me when you left? The last thing I said to you both was don't do anything crazy.'

'I only know what he told me Krystal. He went back to ask him something else and Donaghy pulled a gun on him.'

Although he was dubious about his brother's account of events, as far as Earl was concerned he was telling his sister the truth, because that was what Jethro had told him. He hadn't changed his mind at all and given him permission to go back and kill Donaghy. He had more brains than that. Jethro had only said he was going back because he'd forgotten to ask him something.

'We both know that Donaghy wouldn't have had the balls to draw a gun. I doubt if his weapon ever saw daylight did from the first day they pinned a badge on the fat jerk. Do you really think he would've pulled it on a psycho like your brother. Jethro's lying and you know it. And what's more he's gonna get us all collared. I swear to you Earl, if he wasn't our brother I'd tell you to whack him. He's a fucking liability. Where's the body?'

Jethro could hear the outburst and stood quivering next to Earl.

'Weighted down in the water at the bottom of the dock,' Earl said quietly.

'Well let's hope it stays weighted down then, because if it doesn't and it floats up the shit's really gonna hit the fan. This wasn't just some hobo your brother's offed. He was a fuckin' policeman. The fact that he was a fat, useless piece of crap won't make a difference to the cops. He was one of 'em, and they ain't gonna let it go easy.'

'I know sis, I'm sorry,' Earl said glancing at Jethro and grimacing at him through gritted teeth. 'I should've kept a closer watch on him'.

'Damn right you should. Well from now on you don't let him out of your fucking sight. I'm not sure about anything now. Did Barclay kill Tyrone or not, and is he dead or not? I just don't know what to think any more. So, Earl, this is what you do. Stay down there a while longer in case Barclay shows up. Because if he is alive I'll bet you a dime to a dollar he's gonna be looking for some sort of revenge. And if you do find him, don't kill him. Tell him I want to speak to him. Give him my cell number. That's unless Donaghy's body floats up. Then you hightail it out of Chicago.'

'Where should we go?'

'Any-fucking- where! I don't give a shit. As long as you stay the hell away from me. Wait till I tell you to come here, because that body will have Jethro's trade-mark all over it, and I don't want him nowhere near me.'

'OK.'

'And Earl?'

'Yes Krystal.'

'This time, keep that brainless brother of yours under control. I'm holding you responsible.'

'Yes Krystal.'

22.45 Saturday 16th September 1995. Washington.

Barclay cursed as he drove away from the Washington suburbs. He had no idea what the police were doing at the Weiss's house. Neither could he be certain that he hadn't been spotted. And even if he had, they might not have recognised him without his hair and beard. It could have been only a coincidence that Riley had directed the cops attention in his direction, but he wasn't prepared to take the gamble and hang round to find out. He was certain that the police hadn't followed him, so he kept his speed down to avoid being pulled up by an over-zealous traffic cop.

He also couldn't be sure that the cop didn't get the number. He'd have to stop soon in a quiet unlit road and grab another number plate from a parked car. He should have asked Cassidy to make him some spares. That man could turn his little hands to anything. He cursed his own stupidity for not thinking of it.

Once again his plans had somehow been stymied by the Weiss and Riley partnership. But instead of it putting him off, it only made him more determined to complete his mission and exact some sweet revenge.

Back at the Weiss house Abbey was frantic.

'Do you think it was Barclay?' she asked Mike Riley anxiously.

'I can't be sure Abbey. It's pretty dark out there now and he wasn't parked directly under a street-light, so it was difficult to see who was inside the car, but there was definitely a large man sitting in it. We couldn't see enough of the number plate either. The cop radioed in to see if any other patrol cars were nearby that could maybe approach from the other end of the road but by the time one arrived he'd driven away.'

'It was Jake,' Nathan said. 'I'm sure of it. The car has gone, and so have my shivers. I'm not going mad. It's too much of a coincidence.'

'Listen guys,' Mike said, 'I've arranged for the patrol car to be outside all night. Assuming that it was Barclay, I doubt that he would dare to come back now that he thinks we've seen him, but I'm not prepared to take that chance. And I don't think that you two should either. Nathan, if I hadn't retired yet, you would still outrank me, but I wouldn't be pulling rank on you as anything to do with law enforcement. I'd be doing so as a friend. You're not staying here. You were coming to Chicago for my party next Thursday anyway. So come tomorrow instead. We've got room at our place. You can stay with me and Rita for a few days. You'll be safe there and we can work out what to do. What do you say?' The two men looked at Abbey questioningly.

She nodded. 'OK,' she said.

'Thanks Mike,' said Nathan, 'if you're sure.'

'One minute,' said Abbey. We're forgetting something. Lionel is coming to stay with us in a few days.'

'Whose Lionel?' Mike asked.

'He's my cousin in London,' Nathan said. 'He's coming here to visit. I was going to ask you if he could join us at your party on Thursday. You've probably heard of him. Back in the day he was known as El Lion.'

'Shut the front door! El Lion is your family?'

'Yeah, he's a cousin who I've just reconnected with.'

'No problem Nathan, we've got plenty of room at home since the kids all left. Call him and tell him to come to Chicago instead.'

'Are you sure Mike, he's bringing his wife as well?'

'Sure I'm sure. Good, that's settled then,' said Mike. 'Now, if you don't mind I suggest that we all get some rest. We've got a long drive tomorrow.'

'Follow me Mike,' Nathan said, 'I'll show you to your room.' He turned to Abbey, and gave her a hug and a kiss on the cheek.

'Please try not to worry honey. I promise you, everything will be OK. We'll get him.' He headed up the stairs with Mike following behind him.

But sleep didn't come easily for any of them and at five o'clock in the morning, when Mike went downstairs, he found Abbey and Nathan sitting at the kitchen table, each of them nursing a cup of coffee.

'You couldn't sleep either then?'

'No,' they both said in unison.

'So let's get ready and hit the road then,' said Mike. 'We're going to be driving for most of the day, so the earlier we get started the better. I've got enough room for all of us in my car so we can all go in that. There's no point in taking two vehicles. You can put your bags in my trunk and leave your car here.'

Nathan agreed that it made more sense for them to travel together. They quickly dressed, loaded Mike's car and were soon on their way.

On the drive back from Washington, Barclay thought about nothing else other than what to do next. He was worried that he'd been spotted by Riley at the Weiss's house, so he decided to temporarily divert his focus of attention away from Nathan and to re-group. Other people had also been responsible for the failure of his plans and he would pay them some attention instead. So during the early hours of the morning, he had broken into the Chicago Cancer Clinic through a rear door in the basement car park. Now, he sat in Professor Grant's office awaiting his arrival. As much as he was certain that since he was there last and stole Grant's files, the professor would have put stronger security measures in place. Yet he still tried to access the computer. Not that anything on it was any use to him now. More out of morbid curiosity really, and to pass the time. Sure enough, it was password protected. Barclay didn't possess the skills to break it, so he didn't bother to try. He just sat there patiently, with a silenced Beretta pistol on his lap, waiting for the professor to arrive. He didn't have to wait long. At 8.55 Grant walked into his office and stared open mouthed at the huge figure of Barclay, a man who he believed to be dead, sitting in *his* chair, behind *his* desk, in front of *his* computer.

'What are you doing here?' he gasped.

'What's the problem prof? Seen a ghost have you? Sit down,' Barclay growled, pointing with the gun at the chair in front of the desk. Grant warily sat down, never taking his eyes off the pistol.

'What do you want Barclay?' he said. 'You've already stolen my files. There's nothing else here for you.'

'Yes, you're right, I did, and I know that Grant. But we both also know that you've got them back now don't we? And that you helped that cop Riley and the snot-nosed kid West, or Weiss as his real name is, didn't you?'

Grant looked a Barclay like he was mad. 'What did you expect me to do Barclay? You brought a trumped up patient to my clinic, under false pretences. You killed one of my security guards, you broke into my office and took my life's work. And then, as if that wasn't enough, you killed one of my nurses. An innocent young girl who was no danger to you at all.'

'Yeah, well, she wasn't that innocent. When I shot her she was buck naked, banging that "trumped up patient", who also happened to be a friend of mine, and who thanks to you, is dead. So now you've got to get yours. And then they're gonna get theirs.'

Barclay lifted the Beretta out of his lap and pointed it straight at Grant's face. Seeing the pistol in such close Grant's eyes bulged. 'Wait, I had nothing to do with that,' he pleaded. 'Look, Barclay, why kill more innocent people? It's not going to bring your friend back. You said it yourself, we've got the formula back now. We can hopefully us it to cure thousands of people of a horrible disease. Riley's not even a policeman anymore. He's retired now. And anyway, the whole world thinks you are dead. Nobody has to ever know that you're still alive. You could disappear. So what's the point?'

Barclay arched an eyebrow. 'Riley's retired?'

'Yes, a few weeks ago. The murders and theft from here was his last case.'

'Interesting. A man who was a cop for so many

years. He must be having a retirement party then. Or has he had it already?

The professor sat there tight lipped. He realised that he had already said too much.

'I'll take that as a no then,' Barclay said. 'And I'll bet you've been invited. After all you were the subject of his last successful case. So when and where is it Grant? Tell me and I might let you live.'

Barclay reached across with his left hand and roughly grabbed Grant by his shirt collar. With his right he shoved the pistol hard against Grant's nose. 'Tell me professor, or my ugly face will be the last one you see.'

Grant cried out in pain and squeezed his watering eyes shut. In almost a whisper he said, 'It's this Thursday, at O'Halloran's bar. But you won't get near it. There'll be policemen everywhere. Don't be a fool Barclay. Just please leave, I won't tell anybody you were here, I promise.'

'Thanks for that prof. No, I'm, sure you won't,' Barclay said as he pulled the trigger and blew the back of Grant's head off. Grant was thrown backwards and as the chair toppled over from the force he crashed with it to the floor. Then Barclay lifted up a bag which he had brought with him and left on the floor behind the desk. He removed a block of plastic explosive which was taped to a timer. He set the timer to ten minutes, placed the device on the desk and made his way from the clinic out the same door through which he had entered. Emerging into the car park he got into his car and calmly drove away. He parked a few blocks down and waited and watched. Five minutes later Grant's office exploded, taking the basement and much of the ground floor with it. Plumes of smoke swirled through smashed windows and the decimated front entrance. Passers-by were cut by flying glass. Cars screeched to a halt while others didn't manage to stop in time and smashed into one another. Alarms sounded from every direction. There was complete mayhem. Barclay grinned maliciously and drove away from the pandemonium.

"Part one complete." He thought *"Now for the rest of them."*

11.00 Monday 18th September 1995. Chicago.

Mike Riley's wife Rita answered a knock on the door. She was tall and slim with long flowing jet black hair. She was a few years younger than Riley, always immaculately dressed and made up, whatever the time of day or night. When she opened the door two of Mike's former colleagues were standing there. The looks on their faces told her that they hadn't come for a social visit. She started to panic, then she quickly gathered her thoughts and remembered with relief that not only had Mike retired, but he was safely upstairs in bed, having slept late after the long drive the night before.

'Hi John, Les, how are you?'

'We're fine thanks Rita. You OK?'

'I'm fine, what can I do for you boys?' She didn't like Curtis and Saunders. She had always felt that they were a bit lazy and was relieved that her husband no longer had to depend on them to watch his back.

'Mike around?' John asked.'

'Actually he's asleep…………..'

'I'm here Rita,' Mike said from behind her as he walked down the stairs. 'I guess you're here about the bombing. I just heard it on the radio.'

'Bombing? What bombing?' Rita asked, alarmed. She turned around to face Mike. Nathan and Abbey were behind him.

'Come on in boys,' Mike said.

The cops walked in and they all went into the living room.

'I'll get some coffee on,' Rita said.

'Guys,' said Mike, 'this is Nathan Weiss and his wife Abbey. They came up with me from Washington yesterday.'

'Yeah,' Les Curtis said. 'I recognise you Mister Weiss. You're CIA, right?'

'That's me, one and the same,' said Nathan, smiling.

'Mind if I ask why you're here in Chicago?' John Saunders asked.

'He's here as my guest John, I'll explain that later. First tell me why you're here?'

Les was the senior of the two detectives, so he answered.

'Well Mike, as you said you heard that the cancer clinic blew up this morning. Professor

Grant died along with four of his staff and one of the security guards. Passers-by were badly hurt by flying debris and one was killed by a car which went out of control and ran up on to the sidewalk. It was like a battle scene there. It's very early days but it's looking like the explosion wasn't an accident. We're here because the clinic was involved in the last case you were working on. We were just wondering if you might have any ideas, maybe throw some light on it. The truth is, we'd like to see if we can come up with anything before the Feds get here and take over.'

Abbey, visibly shocked at the news of the death of her former boss dabbed at her eyes which had filled with tears. Nathan put a consoling arm around her. He turned to Mike.

'Mike, it's Barclay isn't it?'

'We can't be sure of that Nathan,' Mike said.

'Hold on a moment. He's dead though Mike. You guys popped him at the docks didn't you?' Les said.

Rita came back with the coffee. 'Barclay's alive?' she said. How can that be?'

'Ok, look, everybody,' Mike said, 'let's just all

calm down and take a breath. Then I'll explain about Barclay, and why Nathan and Abbey are here.'

Over the next few minutes Mike Riley told Rita and the two cops what Nathan had been sensing about Barclay, about the chills and why he believed that he was still alive. The two cops looked sceptically at each other.

'I must admit I was dubious at first,' Mike said looking apologetically across at Nathan. 'But after last night, and again this morning I'm starting to believe it myself. It's too much of a damn coincidence for my liking.'

'Well I agree that we can't rule anything out Mike,' John said. 'But it's a bit of a stretch isn't it. First Barclay being alive, and second him coming back here to blow the clinic up. I mean, what does he stand to gain by it?'

'That's the whole point John.' Nathan said. 'He's an absolute and complete psychopath. He doesn't think like a normal person. He's out for revenge. Mike didn't finish telling you but the reason we're here is because I'm convinced he was outside our house last night. We were coming up for Mike's retirement party anyway so Mike suggested that we came here a few days earlier and had a bit of a vacation at the same time. I'm telling you guys that explosion was caused by Barclay. Somehow he survived when I shot him. It looks like he's laid low since then, until he was ready. He blew up the clinic and I don't think he's going to stop there.'

'So what do we do Mike?' Les said.

'Why are you asking me?' Mike said. 'I'm retired. I'm out. You've got a new boss now.'

'I know that Mike.' Les said. 'But have you got any ideas?'

'Only the routines that you guys already know and follow. Ask around, put his face everywhere, TV, newspapers. The only other targets he could be going for are sitting in front of you now. You can put a cruiser outside my front door if you want. Nathan and I will watch each other's backs.'

'What about your retirement party?' John asked. Are you still going ahead with that.'

'You bet your skinny ass I am.' Mike said. 'I worked damned hard for that clock, and no-one's gonna stop me getting it, not even that psychopath Barclay. That's if he is still alive and we haven't got another lunatic on the loose.'

Les grinned. 'How do you know we've bought you a clock?'

Mike grinned back. 'Because I know you poor saps haven't got the imagination to think of anything else to buy. Go on guys get outa here. Go and catch the bastard.'

The detectives finished their coffee, said their goodbyes and left.

'Are you seriously thinking of going ahead with it Mike?' Nathan said.

'I guess,' Mike said.

'Well,' Nathan said 'if you're sure, it might be the perfect way to draw him out. If we make enough noise about it he's bound to hear. That's if he doesn't know already.'

'Oh I get it,' said Mike, 'you want to paint a target on my back do you? And yours for that matter.'

'Mike the pub will be full of cops. He won't get anywhere near you or me. And we can position enough guys all around the area who'll spot him if he comes within a half a mile of us. They'll be on him like a rash before he even knows they're there.'

'I suppose it could work. One thing's for certain, I'm not letting him frighten me off. And it's still three days away anyway. You never know, we might even catch him by then.'

'I don't like it Mike,' Rita said. 'It's too dangerous.'

'I agree with Rita.' Abbey said.

'Don't worry girls.' Mike said with a mischievous grin, 'It'll be fine. If you're worried you don't have to come to the party. You can both stay here and keep each other company.'

'If you think I'm going to let all those colleagues of yours tell you what they really think of you and not be there to hear them then you've got another think coming Mike Riley.' Rita laughed.

'What about you Abbey?' Nathan asked.

'Well I can't let Rita go on her own can I?'

'That's it then, it's settled.' Riley said. Now let's all relax and enjoy each other's company for a few weeks. Nathan, when did you say your cousin is coming?'

'Tomorrow, around mid-day. I got a message to him telling him to come to Chicago instead of Washington. I'm picking up a car from the local office tomorrow.'

'No need, Nathan, you can take mine.'

'No, its OK thanks, Mike. It's probably best if I've got my own wheels while we're here.'

'OK then, if you're sure. Well, listen, this afternoon I'm going to check over O'Halloran's, just to make some final arrangements. Fancy coming with?'

'Sure, why not?'

Riley grinned broadly, 'Great, say, why don't we all go?'

Seeing nods of agreement all round Riley said happily, 'Wonderful, that's agreed then.'

12.00 Monday 18th September. Chicago.

Earl and Jethro were still in Chicago. There had been no sign of Barclay, and there had been no news of any gruesome discoveries at the docks, so it would appear that Donaghy's bloated body was still on the harbour bed, keeping the fish and the worms happily occupied. Earl had spoken to Krystal the evening before and she had told them to give up the search for Barclay and to come home the following morning. That was until the brothers heard the news about the explosion at the clinic. Earl immediately called Krystal.

'It has to be Barclay,' she said excitedly. 'I told you didn't I. And I'll bet the cop who collared him is next on his list. What did you say his name is?'

'Riley, Mike Riley,' Earl said. Donohue said that he retired and he's having a party at a bar in town, on the 21st. That's this Thursday.'

'Then take my word that's where Barclay's going to be.' Krystal said. 'I'll bet he'll be staking it out as well, to work out the best way of getting to Riley. So you boys do the same, around the clock, starting now.'

'Krystal, what do you want us to do if we find him?'

'I told you, I want to speak to him. I wanted you to bring him to me but I doubt now that he will let that happen. So give him my number and tell him to call me to set up a meet with him, face to face. Then I'll be able to judge for myself if he killed Tyrone. You know me, I can always smell out a liar.'

'And if he did kill Tyrone?'

'I'll decide at the time. I'll either kill him myself, or if I'm in a good mood I might change my mind and let Jethro have him, ' she said ominously.

'And what if he didn't?'

'I'll cross that bridge when I come to it. Now go and find him.'

Krystal disconnected, leaving Earl wondering what the hell she was up to.

16.00 Monday 18th September 1995. Chicago.

Driving a black ford Mustang Cobra which he'd boosted from a supermarket car park and to which he'd fixed another pair of his growing collection of stolen number plates, Barclay cruised down South Canal Street. He checked out O'Halloran's bar as he drove past. He was wearing a blue baseball cap, with the peak pulled down as far as it could go without impairing his vision. The collar of his polo shirt was turned up and obscured the sides of his face.

O'Halloran's occupied the ground floor of a double fronted building on the corner of Union Street. Ornately decked out in black and gold with the name spelled out in big green letters across the windows, it could be seen from several blocks away. At night, the Irish folk music which was belted out by the resident band carried just as far.

As he drove past, Barclay's attention was caught by a blue sedan parked a little way up from the corner. He spotted two African American guys sitting in the front of the vehicle. They weren't talking to each other. Instead they were just watching the traffic as it drove past. Barclay couldn't believe his eyes. He jerked his head around to have a second look. If he hadn't known better he would have sworn that the man behind the wheel was Tyrone. But he knew it couldn't be. He'd seen him bleed out in the warehouse. He pulled the car up a few blocks away and walked back towards the bar, being careful to keep his head down. He was sure that every cop in the district carried a picture of him and had been told to be on the lookout. He circled around the block and came up behind the bar. From a doorway fifty yards away he could get a better view of the two men and then it dawned on him who they were. Tyrone's brothers.

"Now what are they doing here?" he thought. *"Looking for me I guess. But why?"*

Hiding his gun behind his back he walked up to the back of the car, keeping out of the line sight of the wing mirror. Then he darted across the road and in one fluid movement he opened the door and slid in the back seat. Jethro tried to swivel around and draw his knife, but Barclay pistol-whipped him across his ear. Jethro yelped in pain as Barclay grabbed his wrist and twisted it sharply so that the knife fell to the carpeted floor of the footwell. Before Earl could react

Barclays gun was already pointing at him. It had all happened in a matter of two seconds.

'Fuck you man,' whinged Jethro.

Earl just stared at him. 'I see that you're still alive then Jake.' he said.

'Yep. Very much so Earl. What are you doing here?'

'Looking for you.'

"And what do you two low life pieces of crap want with me?'

'We want to know what happened to Tyrone, that's what,' sneered Jethro, holding his hand to his ear.

'He got what he deserved, that's what happened to him. He ratted me out to the cops. My boss, actually, my ex-boss now, killed him in the warehouse. Shame really, I'd have liked to have done it myself, but Kirkpatrick shot him before I had the chance.'

Earl sat there mulling over this new information, before saying, 'Tyrone would never rat anybody out Jake, specially you. You two worked together for Christ's sake. There must have been more to it than that.'

'I don't give a fuck Earl, whatever the reason.

He was ready to give me up to the cops. So, I'll say it again, I didn't kill him, but he had it coming.'

Jethro dived forward, trying to reach his knife. This time Earl slapped him across the back of the head, bringing another squeal from his younger brother. 'Be still Jethro, Earl shouted. 'You ain't gonna get the better of this man. All your gonna get is a bullet in the back of your head.'

'Listen to your brother Jethro,' Barclay said coldly. If you move again I'll shoot your brother in the face, then I'll tear your head off and shove it up your ass. You got that?'

'Yeah, I got that.'

'Now,' Barclay said. 'At the moment I've got no beef with you two. So I'll ask you one last time. What are you doing here?'

'We thought you'd killed Tyrone,' Earl said, 'so Krystal sent us to find out what went down. We was told you didn't and when we told her she still wanted us to check it out.'

'Who told you I didn't kill him.'

'A cop who heard the whole story.'

'And that still wasn't good enough for your

sister?'

'No,' Earl said. 'She wants to speak with you herself.'

Barclay thought for a moment. Strange as it seemed, he was intrigued.

'Give me her number,' he said.

'Earl slowly reached into an inside pocket, brought out his cell-phone and read out the number which Barclay put into his phone.

Without another word he got out of the car to make his way back to the Mustang.

Earl shoved the car into drive, screeched out of Union Street, into South Canal Street and roared up the road toward the highway and out of Chicago.

As Barclay walked quickly past O'Halloran's, if he'd glanced through the window, he would have seen Mike and Nathan inside. Nathan was standing next to Mike while he went over a few details with Ray, the owner. Rita and Abbey sat at a table chatting over a cup of coffee.

The establishment was a huge rectangular room decked out with circular oak tables and sturdy oak chairs with wicker backs. Four large rustic candelabras hung from the ceiling. The bar itself, also oak, stretched most of the length of one wall. It was famed for displaying one of the best stocked collections of Irish Whiskey and other booze in Chicago, and was trimmed along the top with an ornate gilt rail. Irish flags and sporting memorabilia adorned the walls and to emphasize the Gaelic theme the floor was tiled in white, green and orange squares.

Suddenly Nathan, who had been gazing around admiring the ambiance felt a chill down his spine. He grabbed Mike's arm.

'What is it Nathan? What's up?'

'Barclay?' Nathan said, quietly not wanting Abbey to hear. His face was as white as a ghost's. 'He's here, I can feel it.'

'Are you OK mate' Ray asked. Should I get you some water?'

Nathan didn't answer, he walked quickly towards the door, with Mike following. Mike was about to reach for his service weapon, then remembered that being retired, he was no longer armed.

Abbey stood up.

'Nathan, where are you going, what's the matter?'

'Nothing honey, stay there with Rita, I'll be back in a moment.'

He opened the door and looked out. 'Let me go first,' Mike said, edging in front of Nathan.

The two men stepped out onto the street, looked up and down, saw nothing. Nathan scanned along South Canal Street, and saw nothing. Mike darted around the junction to look up Union Street, with the same result. Nothing. Barclay had already turned the corner and was in his car. He drove away through the back street, out of sight of Nathan and Mike. They stepped back into the bar. Nathan was wearing a mystified look on his face.

Abbey came up to them. 'It's Barclay isn't it? He's here isn't he?'

'No, of course not,' Nathan said, before Mike could answer. 'I just felt a bit queasy, that's all. I needed to get some some air.'

Mike took Nathan's lead. 'Yeah, that's all it was. You're OK now though ain't you Nathan?'

'Sure, I'm fine.'

'Good, let's finish up with Ray and we can get home.'

They walked back to the bar and Nathan said

quietly, 'Thanks for backing me up Mike. I don't want to scare Abbey or Rita, and I don't want to screw up the plans for your special night either. But I'm not crazy Mike,' Nathan insisted. 'He was here. Barclay was definitely here. I was right the other night outside our house, and I'm right now.'

'OK, OK. Maybe he's heard about the party and he's staking the place out. But don't worry. As you said, on the night we'll have the place surrounded by cops. My pals will take it in turns to keep watch. He won't get near the place. And if he does, all the better, because we'll get him, once and for all. Come on let's get going. I need a drink, and it's free at home.'

17.30 Monday 18th September. Chicago.

Back in his room at the motel five miles out of Chicago, Jake Barclay was studying a map and smiling cruelly to himself as he planned his route and the assault on O'Halloran's bar.

He took out his cell-phone and punched in a number.

A deep gravelly voice answered.

'Stanley's.'

'Foreman, it's Jake, how's it hanging?'

Like most people Stanley Foreman was never overjoyed to hear from Jake Barclay. He'd learned when they served together in Vietnam that Jake was a loose cannon. More than that every time that he'd spoken to Jake over the years it spelled trouble. He operated his business very close to the wind, dealing in stolen vehicles, either selling them on to his criminal friends to use on heists, or breaking them up and using the parts on repair jobs. He ran it very successfully out of a lock-up off Union Street, not far from where Jake had seen Earl and Jethro. It was a typical mechanic's workshop. A rectangular building with workbenches cluttered with tools along two walls and off to one side a hydraulic ramp hovered over a pit. The smell of grease and oil assailed anybody who entered, and mixed with cigarette smoke it floated in the air like the Chicago mist which hung over the city outside. As well as his snide personality, one of the main factors which contributed to his never being able to hold onto staff was that he never wanted to pay a fair day's dollar for a hard day's work. So eventually he gave up trying and for the last two years he had worked alone. He was as crooked as a three dollar bill. And Stanley Foreman knew that Barclay knew it. So, Barclay had him exactly where he needed him. And he needed him now.

'I've been worse Jake. What can I do for you?'

'I need your place on Thursday, in the afternoon and all night. Make sure it's cleared out. I don't want no-one around. I'll be bringing in a Crown Vic. I need you to dress it in decals to look like a Chicago PD Cruiser. Have false plates ready as well. Later that night I'll be bringing it back to have the decals taken off and the original plates put back on so I can drive it away.'

Foreman was silent on the other end of the phone.

'Are you hearing me Foreman?' Jake barked.

'Sure Jake, but you're only giving me a few days. Where am I gonna get the PD decals from?'

'Use your imagination Foreman?'

'Listen, Jake,' Foreman pleaded. 'Just hold on a minute. Why don't I just steal a cop car? I can hide it here till Thursday and change the plates. When you've done whatever you need it for, bring it back and I'll break it up and sell the parts for scrap. That way you won't have to pay me nothing and it'll save a lot of trouble.'

'Where are you gonna boost a cop car from Foreman? They're not exactly gonna be sitting around the streets waiting for you with a sign on them saying "boost me" are they?'

'Stanley Foreman laughed. There are two cops, fat lazy fuckers who usually leave their car parked around the corner at night. They sit in the café all nice and warm, drinking coffee and stuffing their faces with doughnuts while they wait for a call. From where they sit they can't even see their wagon. I'll have it away and hidden at my place before they can say "what the fuck are you doing?"

'Are you sure about this Foreman? If you screw up and I'm left without wheels all my plans go down the toilet.'

'Of course I'm sure Jake.' Foreman said. 'It'll be a piece of cake. To tell you the truth I'm surprised you didn't think of that first. You must be losing your touch.' As soon as the words left his mouth Foreman regretted it. A chill went down his spine while he waited for the rebuke.

After what seemed like an age Barclay said. 'OK, if you're sure. But there's a couple of other things you'll have to do as well.'

Relieved to have got away with it Foreman said, 'Sure, what's that Jake?'

'You remember that midget Cassidy I sent you to adapt his Queen Vic so that he could drive it? You souped it up as well. Can you do the same with the cop car? I need him to do a job and somehow the little fucker drives like a man possessed. I'd back him to win the Indy 500 in it.'

'Sure, that's dead easy Jake, it's only fitting a

few cables and resetting the carburettor. It's a piece of cake. In fact I've probably still got the measurements in a drawer somewhere.'

'Good, I might tweak your plan a little bit, but that's more or less what we'll do. Oh, and Foreman, you're gonna have to boost a dumpster truck as well.'

18.00 Monday 18th September. Albuquerque.

Lance Cassidy answered his cell-phone.

'Cassidy,' Jake said. 'It's me.'

Cassidy didn't need to be told who "me" was. He'd recognise that voice anywhere.

'I've got a job for you,' Barclay said.'

'Already? I only just set you up with a load of new docs.'

'No, not that. It's a driving job I'm going to need you to do for me, this Thursday night. So don't go making any plans.'

Cassidy owned what was probably the only Ford Crown Victoria which had been specially adapted with hand controls to allow for the fact that his feet couldn't reach the pedals. It was an ex-police vehicle which had been wrecked in a pile up during a chase and he'd purchased from the breakers. Jake had recommended him to Stanley Foreman, and he paid him handsomely to restore it. The souped up 190 horsepower engine was so fast that it could, if necessary, outrun almost anything else on the road. Lance drove it like he was born to it. He regularly raced it, and unless they had prior knowledge, anyone watching him wouldn't have had a clue about his disability. But it was his pride and joy. He didn't want to risk wrecking it by using it as a getaway car, and he was sure that's what Barclay meant when he said, "a driving job."

'In my car?'

'No, in one modified the same as yours which Foreman is getting ready for you. It'll be just the same as driving your own car, maybe even better.'

'What sort of job Jake? I don't want to get myself involved.'

'You are already involved Cassidy.' Barclay barked. 'You're tied to me like a puppy strapped on a leash. And if you've got any doubts about doing what I tell you, here's a question for you. You're still living with your mother ain't you? And don't lie to me cos I've checked, and I've seen that nice picture you keep on your desk of the two of you together.'

The question surprised Cassidy and he didn't answer. So Barclay took it as a yes.

'Good. Well if you want her to stay alive and well so she can still tuck you into your little bed at night, you'll do exactly as I tell you. I'll be in touch with the details in a day or so. And don't go blabbing to anyone either, or I'll be burying the both of you in the same hole. Don't forget, Thursday night. Keep your cell on. You'll be picking me up at my motel. I'll give you the address when I call you to come and get me.'

Barclay disconnected. Cassidy was left shaking so much he dropped the phone onto his desk. He lowered his head into his hands and cried.

Next Barclay called the number Earl had given him that afternoon.

'I hear you wanted to speak to me.'

Krystal recognised the voice immediately. 'Nice to hear from you Jake.'

'What do you want me for Kitten?'

'Wow, it's a long time since you called me that,' Krystal said. 'I want to see you Jake. I've got something to discuss with you, but not over the phone.'

Barclay laughed. 'If you only want to ask me if I killed Tyrone a phone conversation will do just fine Krystal. And the answer is no. I didn't. If you don't believe me then that's your problem.'

'If I *only* want to ask you if you killed Tyrone Jake,' Krystal shouted down the phone. 'We're talking about my brother here, so it's a damn sight more than *only* Jake. Earl called me after your little chat in the car this morning. He told me what you said. Seems to me that if you thought he ratted you out to the cops you had a good enough reason to kill him. I want to look you in the eye while you tell me you didn't. Then I'll tell you whether I believe you or not. And if I don't, it'll be your fucking problem.

Probably your last problem.'

Barclay was caught off guard by the rebuke. Listening to Krystal rant at him he understood why all three of her brothers were in awe of her. Well the two that were left anyway. He admired her toughness.

'You know what Krystal. I'll meet you. I'll even drive the 800 odd miles to New York. But not till the end of the week. I've got some unfinished business to take care of first.'

'Riley?' Krystal asked.

'Yeah, Riley.' Jake said. 'He fucked things up for me. I'd have been able to disappear to a nice retirement in the sun if he hadn't got involved. And that so called brother of mine. He's got it coming as well.'

'Well I don't care what you do Jake. If you don't get killed getting your revengeful rocks off in the process, then give me another call. We can meet, and if I'm happy with what you tell me I've got something for you. It might not mean that you can retire, but you could have a very good life. I'll be here when you're ready.'

Krystal broke the connection.

Jake smiled. *"Get this week over he thought to*

himself. Take a trip to New York. Maybe things aren't so bad after all."

11.20 Tuesday 19th September. Chicago O'Hare Airport.

Nathan and Abbey stood at arrivals waiting for Lionel and Rebecca to come through. When they appeared Nathan recognised Lionel immediately. They shook hands warmly and introduced their wives to each other.

'Follow me,' Nathan said, 'The car's just outside.'

'Special parking privileges being CIA then,' Lionel joked as he pushed the trolley along behind Nathan.

'Actually it's not mine. I had to commandeer one when I got to Chicago. Mine's back in Washington.'

'Yes,' Lionel said, 'I was going to ask you about that. Why the sudden change of plan?'

Nathan said over his shoulder. 'We received an unexpected invitation from a friend and when we told him you were coming to stay, he kindly extended it to you guys as well.' Then seeing that Abbey and Rebecca were chatting away already and getting to know one another he turned and spoke in an undertone to Lionel. 'I'll explain the real reason to you later. I don't want to worry the girls.'

They put the luggage in the trunk and drove back to the Riley's house. After the introductions and the usual pleasantries and references to Lionel's' famous history, Rita and Abbey showed Rebecca the house. Nathan led Lionel to the garden, and Riley followed. Nathan then explained to Lionel why they had moved to Chicago. Lionel looked from Nathan to Mike and said, 'I read up on the Barclay case on the way out here. And I understand that the local clinic was blown up and they fancy him for that as well. Well, if he's not dead then it makes sense that he would be the number one suspect. And I get it about the shivers Nathan, I really do. He's your brother after all, which makes it all the more feasible. So, what's the plan?'

Mike Riley cut in. 'We don't have one, other than to be ultra-diligent, to watch our backs, and not to let the girls see that we're concerned. A patrol is going past this house every fifteen minutes. If he's watching here, which I actually doubt, he'll see that anyway.'

'And you're going ahead with your party?' Lionel asked.

'Yep. No-one's going to talk me out of that. I've earned it, and anyway the place will be full of cops. If he's crazy enough to try anything, we'll get the bastard.'

'I sure hope so.'

'Right, ' Mike said, trying to lighten things up. 'My throats drier than a camel's armpit. Let's have a drink.'

The three men went back into the house and Mike rustled some drinks up from the bar.

04.30 Thursday 21st September. Stanley's Workshop, Chicago.

Barclay had stayed put in his motel room for the last two days.

He parked the Mustang a few blocks away and as arranged he arrived at the back door of Stanley's workshop and knocked quietly. Foreman furtively opened the door.

'It's not far to the café, we can walk there ,' he said, 'then we'll only have one vehicle to bring back.' He spread his arms expansively. 'By the way, how do you like the dumpster truck?'

Taking up half of the workshop was a large grey dumpster truck which he'd taken from the local council yard only a few hours earlier.

'Those idiots just leave them parked there, with the keys in them. And,' he said proudly, 'the gates to the yard only have a stupid little padlock on them that any kid could pick.'

'It'll do,' Barclay said, unimpressed. 'Are you carrying?'

'No,' Foreman said, surprised at the question. He hated guns, and hadn't handled one since coming back from Vietnam. Then remembering who he was speaking to, he asked 'Why? Should I be?'

Barclay just sneered back at him derisively. 'Come on, let's get this done. I want to be back in my motel room and getting some sleep. Big night tonight,' he said ominously. You remember the plan?'

'Sure Jake, no problem.'

'Repeat it to me then.'

Foreman recited the instructions which Barclay had been over with him on the phone the day before, as if he was rehearsing lines in a play. 'As soon as you drive past the junction where I'll be parked waiting in the dumpster, you'll pull up, I scoot it across the street to block it, jump down from the passenger door and get in the back of the cop car and Cassidy drives it back here. I run in to raise the shutter and he drives straight in, then I drop it down.'

'That's right, but you don't put the lights on till it's down. Cassidy and I will change and go straight out the back to where the Cassidy's car will be parked. You stay to finish what you have do in here, then open the roller shutters as usual at 9. OK?'

'Sure. You wanna tell me what you'll be doing while I'm waiting in the dumpster truck?' he asked nervously.

'Nah, you don't need to know, and anyway the less you know the better. Now, let's get going.'

Fat Joe's Sandwich Bar was just around the corner. As Foreman had predicted the two policeman were secured inside, and were sitting at a table with Joe Catchpole, the owner. He was a short and portly middle aged man with thinning hair, a huge bulbous nose and Prince Charlesque sticky-out ears. He'd come to The States from London twenty years ago with the idea of making a fortune as a real estate agent. He'd been told that his English accent would wow the Americans and he naively believed that within no time he would be living a life of luxury. Unfortunately, he hadn't realised that one needed the charisma and the looks, as well as the accent, and he was deficient in both of those departments. But his ambition to retire a wealthy man was still actively beating within him and he regularly sat with the cops who were both coming up to retirement, discussing using their savings and pensions to venture into the property market. The recent dip in property prices meant that there were several opportunities to pick up a few bargains.

The police car was a few doors along the road, and Foreman carried on walking towards it. Jake grabbed his arm and held him back.

'Jake, that's their car,' he whispered. 'That's what we came for.'

'No, leave it, I've got a different idea. We don't have to boost it, we'll just drive it away. Come on.'

Barclay strode into the café, with Foreman behind him.

Catchpole greeted them, 'morning gents, something I can get you?' he said.

'Yes please, two coffees.' said Barclay stepping up to the table and reaching his hand behind him to rest on butt of the pistol nestled in his trouser belt. 'And I'll also have the keys to that cop car outside.'

The two policeman, who had been studying the pages of figures which were spread out on the table in front of them and therefore not paying much attention, now looked up.

Ricky Archibald was a large African American. His bulging chest and pot belly prevented him from sitting close to the table. He recognised Barclay from the picture which had been circulated and his cheerful face turned to one of alarm as he fumbled for his service pistol. Harry Blair, who when they examined his body a day or so later on the mortuary table would simply be described as "a white male, of average height and build," was only a second behind him. But neither of them was fast enough. Barclay brought his silenced Glock out from behind his back and shot them both, "tap-tap" in the head.

'What the fuck Jake, ' Foreman shouted. 'You just blew two cops' brains out. Why the hell did you do that?'

'Well,' Barclay drawled, 'I wouldn't want to get any blood on their shirts now would I?' he said with an attempt at sick humour, 'Anyway, they ain't the first cops I've killed, and now we don't have to boost their car. Take their uniforms off, pants as well, and grab the keys. Move it Foreman, we ain't got all day.' He turned to Joe Catchpole and grinned. 'Hold the coffee willya.'

He said as he brought the Glock up again and shot him in the heart.' Catchpole crashed over the back of the chair and fell into a heap.

'Hand me the bigger shirt and put the other one on,' he ordered Foreman, who stood there with a look of complete bewilderment on his face.

Barclay shrugged into the shirt. It was tight but it just about went over his bulk. The pants were a little short.

'Grab the caps Foreman, come on man, snap out of it willya!'

As soon as they were dressed Barclay searched around for a bag to put their original clothes in. Finding one in the kitchen he stuffed everything in it. Then he went to Catchpole's corpse and searched his pockets for the keys to the café. They were on a clip which was attached to one of his belt loops. He snatched them and walked around switching everything off, including the lights. He turned the sign on the door around to "Closed" and hustled Foreman, who was still shaking, out of the door. He gave a quick furtive look around, pleased to note that there weren't any security cameras directed at the café. He locked it and they walked to the police car.

'Get in and drive away,' he ordered Foreman. 'Nice and slowly. Circle the block a few times and then make your way back to your place.'

'What have you done man?' Foreman wailed. 'We'll both fuckin' fry for that you know.'

'Stop your whining,' Barclay snapped back. 'This way the car won't be reported missing until they realise the cops ain't turned up for duty later tonight. With any luck no-one will be looking for them or their car today. I checked their hands. No wedding bands, so maybe no little ladies waiting for them at home either. Which means that we should be free and clear until tonight. And then, by the time anyone finds them we'll be long gone. And I'll have done what I gotta do in a car that no-one realises has been taken.'

'I ain't so sure man. I don't know what you're planning, but I don't want no more to do with it.'

Foreman winced as he felt Barclay's Glock pressed hard into his ribs,

'You'll do what I fucking tell you Foreman, or I'll blow a hole in you and take you back to the café and dump you with them three. Then I'll go to your house, slit the throats of your wife and kids and take their bodies there to keep yours company. So unless you want that to happen, you'll fix this car up today so Cassidy can drive it. And you'll make sure you're in position in that truck tonight, and do your part of the fucking job. You got that Foreman?' Barclay yelled, leaning right into his ear.

'Yeah, Jake. I've got it,' Foreman said quietly.

'Good, I'm sure the ten grand that'll be coming your way when the job is finished will make you feel a whole lot better about it. Now drive us back to your workshop.'

Foreman doubted that ten grand would be coming his way. *"More likely it's a fucking bullet that will be coming my way,"* he thought. But he also had no doubt that Barclay's threat to his family was real, and it frightened the life out of him. Realising he had no other option but to do what he was told, he drove on without saying another word.

When they got to the workshop and the cop car was safely inside Barclay tipped out the bag which had their clothes in it. They stripped off the uniforms, got dressed, and Barclay said

'Right, see you tonight. Get to work on the car.' He let himself out of the back door and was gone, leaving Foreman to wallow in the misery of his predicament.

At nine o'clock that evening the call that Cassidy had been dreading came through to his cell phone.

'I'm at the Starlight motel. You know it?'

'Yeah,' Lance Cassidy answered. He knew it only too well. It was his regular haunt where he entertained the hookers who hung about outside looking for business.

'Good, be here in thirty minutes. Room 17. Park around the back next to the Mustang. ' The call disconnected.

Cassidy teetered on unsteady legs to his mother's bedroom. He knocked gently on the door and went in. Florrie Cassidy was sitting up in bed reading a romantic novel, which was her favourite pastime. She was eighty years old and frail, with lily-white skin, skeletal arms and wispy white hair. She looked up at him.

'What's up son, you look upset?'

'Nothin' ma, I just gotta go out for a little while, OK? You go to sleep, I won't be long.'

Even with her advancing years and weak body, Florrie Cassidy still had a sharp brain and she sensed that her son was battling with a problem. But she knew that questioning him would only upset him more, so she simply did what many mothers would in the same situation. She just said, 'Ok son, you be careful.'

'I will ma. Don't worry. I'll be back before you know it.'

Lance closed the door and stood on the other side of it for a few seconds, wondering with gloomy trepidation if this would be the last time he would see or speak to his beloved mother.

He walked slowly out of the house to his car, being sure to securely lock the door behind him. When he got in the car he ran his hands lovingly around the steering wheel and over the leather seats. He sighed heavily and drove away to meet the man who frightened him more than anything he had ever before encountered.

He drove slowly to the Starlight Motel, fretting over every mile that passed. As he pulled in next to the Mustang Barclay stepped out of it, walked around to the passenger side of Lance's car, threw open the door and dropped onto the bench seat. He was carrying a heavy looking case which he placed between them.

'Good man, you're on time. Let's go and do this.

When it's done, as long as you've done exactly as I tell you, you and your ma can live a long and healthy life.'

'What is it you want me to do Jake?'

'To drive Lance, just to drive, as only you can.'

'So where are we going now?'

'Foreman's.' Barclay said. 'I've got a little mission I need to do. I can't do it and drive at the same time. That's why I need you. He's modified a cop car the same as he did yours. You gotta drive it for me. Come on man, get going, the clock's ticking.'

Cassidy drove slowly out of the motel forecourt. He turned right and began the twenty minute drive down to Chicago City centre.

His nerves were shredded and jangling. He correctly suspected that Barclay was embarking on some fearful mission and he desperately wanted to protest that he wanted no part of it. But due to Barclay's threat to his mother he daren't argue with the man. He could feel his stomach churning and turning to water. Resigning himself to the fact that he was between a rock and a hard place he drove in silence, chewing on his bottom lip for the rest of the journey. He pulled up to the back of Foreman's place and they both got out of the car.

'Bring that with you, you're going to need it,' Barclay said to Cassidy, pointing to the cushion he sat on to give him enough height to see over the steering wheel. Barclay hefted out the case and tapped on the workshop door. Foreman opened it a crack and peering out he saw both of them standing there. He stood aside and they walked in. He closed the door and locked it behind them.

'You know Cassidy here,' Barclay said.

'Sure, hi Lance,' Foreman said. 'how are you doing?'

Cassidy just nodded sadly, and Foreman realised straight away that Lance Cassidy was only there because he was under the same type of threat from Barclay that he was. He liked Cassidy, and sympathised with him. But before he had any time to dwell on it Barclay was already issuing orders.

'Right Foreman, get those uniforms out.'

Foreman went to a cupboard, fished out the uniforms and handed them to Barclay. Barclay took his and handed the other one to Cassidy. 'Right let's get these on and we can be on our way.'

Cassidy looked at Barclay, then at the police car and the penny dropped. They were going to be impersonating police officers. He started to panic. He wanted to scream that this was going too far. How the hell could he, a midget of all things, possibly pass for a policeman? As if he could read Cassidy's mind Barclay said, 'Don't worry little feller, you won't have to get out the car. Come on, get that gear on, we gotta go.' Cassidy ignored the insult. What else could he do?

The two men put the uniforms on.

When Cassidy was ready, the shirt cuffs were trailing on the floor. The pants legs were overlapping his shoes by a good three feet. He looked like a two year old little boy playing dress up in his father's pyjamas. When he put the cap on, even though his head was too big for his own body, it still slipped so far down it obscured half of his face.

Something happened then that neither Cassidy or Foreman had experienced before, or would ever have imagined ever could, and it took both of them completely by surprise. Barclay laughed, but not just a chuckle, but a real belly laugh. His face nearly broke in half, massive shoulders rolled up and down and he bent at the waist to grab his thighs in an effort to control himself. In spite of everything, Stanley Foreman and Lance Cassidy found themselves caught up in the moment and joined in the laughter. But as quick as it had started the moment passed.

'Right,' Barclay said, getting a grip on himself slapping his cap firmly on to his head. 'Time to go. Cassidy, check the car out. It should be set up identical to yours, at least it better had be,' he said glancing threateningly at Foreman.

Cassidy shuffled comically over to the police car, the bottom half of the pants legs dragging beneath his feet, threw in the cushion and hauled himself in. He quickly checked out the controls. Everything was in order. He started the engine. It roared to life as he gunned the gas and then it settled down to a gentle rumble. He looked across to Barclay and nodded.

'Good,' Barclay said. 'OK, Foreman, we're off.

Wait till we've been gone fifteen minutes then move the truck into position where I told you. Stay alert. I'm not sure what time we'll be coming past, but you'll definitely hear us, that I am fucking sure about.'

Picking the case up from the floor where he'd put it down when they came in, Barclay clambered into the passenger seat and put it on the bench seat between him and Cassidy. He slammed the door and pressed the button to lower the passenger door window.

'Lift the shutters up Foreman,' he shouted. Then he turned to Cassidy. 'Turn right out of here onto Union Street, right again onto South Canal Street. Drive down a few blocks, hang a "U" turn and then I'll tell you where to park.'

Cassidy turned up the cuffs of the police uniform shirt so that they didn't impede his access to the specially fitted levers on the steering column. He nodded and had to push back the loosely fitting cap to stop it flapping over his eyes.

They drove out leaving Foreman lowering the shutter and saying to himself 'That's another fine fucking mess you got yourself into Stanley!'

At precisely the time Barclay and Cassidy were driving out of Foreman's workshop Mike Riley was walking past the two uniformed policemen and into O'Halloran's bar arm in arm with Rita and flanked by Nathan, Abbey, Lionel and Rebecca.

The bar was already packed with policemen and women many of whom were in uniform. A loud chorus of cheers and applause greeted Mike as he walked in. He waved his thanks to everybody and went straight across to Les Curtis.

'How we doing he asked?' trying his best not to show any concern.

'Don't worry Mike we got guys on every corner. None of 'em are in uniform and they all know how not to look too obvious so if Barkley shows we'll get him. Just relax and enjoy yourself boss.'

'Thanks Les.' Mike said. He turned round to the crowd and raised his hands to silence everybody.

'First of all,' he said, I want to thank you all for coming. Have a great evening, drink as much as you like, it's Rita's treat.'

Rita puffed out her cheeks and shook her head

as people laughed and heckled.

One called out 'It wouldn't surprise us, Mike, You've not been guilty of buying a round your whole bloody life!' More laughter.

Mike silenced the crowd again. And, in case any of you are wondering who my friends are, on my left here,' he said pointing to Nathan, is the young man who has recently become the youngest ever assistant director of the CIA, Nathan Weiss, and on my right is someone who many of you will know as the sporting hero El Lion, the Olympic champion and World Cup winner Lionel Streat, who is here on a visit. Make them welcome guys they're both very important to me. Now enough of that let's get a few drinks in.

Another cheer went up, A few of the guys started to chant "El Lion, El Lion." Even nearly thirty years later the star of Lionel's fame still shone brightly.

A guy at the back of the room called out, 'Blow me Mike, talk about rent a crowd. How much did you have to pay for them to come?'

The guy's comment was greeted by applause and howls of laughter and he bowed and spread his arms expansively to express his appreciation.

Lionel looked at Nathan with relief.

'For a minute there I was worried Mike was going to say what I do for a living now as well.'

The barman signalled to the musicians on the stage to start playing and they broke into a loud Irish folk song.

Mike, Nathan and Lionel tried to dismiss the potential threat outside and circulated the bar, shaking hands and sharing jokes. But every few minutes they furtively looked around in the direction of the entrance to the bar to make sure that there was no way any unwelcome visitors could intrude.

By now Barclay was in position, parked far enough along the road that he could keep an eye on the entrance but not draw any unwanted attention. Cassidy sat next to him in the driver's seat, silently fretting, not wanting to think about what was going to happen when Barclay decided it was time to make his move.

He got an even better idea of what was about to go down when Barclay reached into the case and brought out an automatic machine pistol and laid it on his lap.

'Oh my dear God, no,' Cassidy groaned.

Barclay ignored him and kept his eyes firmly fixed on the door of O'Halloran's bar.

At ten thirty, inside the bar the party was at full throttle. Mike Riley had completely relaxed, as had everyone except Nathan. Despite Barclay being far enough away that he didn't feel any shivery sensations, he was still regularly glancing around nervously. Abbey nudged him, 'Hey, Nathan, stop being the Assistant Director for one night, please. For me, heh, how about it honey?'

'Of course Abbey, I'm sorry. He lovingly placed his hands on the slight bulge in her stomach, which was now showing the first signs of her pregnancy.

'How are my boys doing?' he asked.

'And how do you know that they are both boys?'

'A father's instinct,' he said smiling.

'Well Mister Weiss,' she said, taking his hand and resting it back on her tummy, 'you've done your bit, but your amazing powers of detection will do you no good in this particular department. Mother nature will decide, and we will all find out in very good time what she has in store for us.' He leaned forward and kissed her softly on the lips.

'That will do for me,' he said. 'I love you Abbey Weiss.'

Mike Riley, who was by now a little worse the wear due to the several beers and bourbon chasers he had imbibed, called out to them from across the other side of the bar.

'Oi you two, get a bloody room!'

As laughter echoed around the room, Les Curtis called, 'OK everyone, time for the boring ass-licking speeches and presentation. Gather round please.'

Another thirty minutes flew by. Rita said a few words about what it had been like over the years being married to a detective. How she fretted when he moved across to homicide. And how she breathed a sigh of relief every time he came home safe and sound.

Les made a nice but surprisingly mostly serious toast, interspersed with the few expected and regular corny jokes about what it was like to work for an Irish boss. But he finished with a sincere wish for Mike and Rita to spend a long and happy retirement together. Then he presented Mike with the clock. Mike opened it and brought the house down when he said, 'A clock, my oh my, what a fuckin' surprise.'

'Mike,' Rita reprimanded, 'watch your language, there's ladies present!'

'Yeah? Where are they Rita?'

Raucous laughter filled the bar, glasses were filled and clinked, and the party continued into the night.

Barclay kept his vigil going. He was assuming that the party-goers would start filing out at around midnight. The later the better as far as he was concerned, less traffic about. He looked around for signs of any obvious cops on the prowl looking for him. If Riley did spot him a few nights ago, then it was likely that he was the chief suspect in the bombing at the clinic. In which case not only would every cop in the city be looking for him, but Riley would have also definitely heightened security around his party.

'Hey Cassidy,' he said, arousing Lance out of his miserable stupor, 'take a discreet look over the street. See the guy standing outside the coffee bar on the corner?'

'Yeah, what about him?'

'You see what he's doing?'

'Standing under the street-light, reading a paper.'

'Doesn't that strike you as strange?' Barclay asked.

'Not especially, why?'

'Because he's outside a coffee bar in the middle of the night. Instead of standing outside, why not go in, sit down comfortably with a cup of coffee and read the paper?'

Cassidy thought for a moment. 'Well maybe he ain't got any money, or maybe he doesn't like coffee. What's your point Jake?'

'My point is, dumbass, that he's on stake out. And he's been watching this car for just a little bit longer than makes me comfortable. Drive around the block and come up in the street behind.'

Cassidy didn't move. He just sat there as if in a trance, looking at the machine pistol.

'Start the fucking car and move away!' Barclay roared.

Cassidy fired up the engine and drove down

South Canal street a block past O'Halloran's and circled back around to come up behind the coffee bar.

'Stop here', Barclay said.

Cassidy pulled the car to a stop. Barclay got out and with surprisingly light steps for such a big man he crept along the sidewalk and looked around the corner. The guy had moved and was looking up South Canal Street, apparently trying to see if Barclay's car had stopped further up. Failing to see it he turned around and was about to speak into a two way radio which he had drawn from his coat pocket when he came face to face with Barclay.

'Looking for me?' Barclay snarled.

Before the guy could even register surprise, Barclay's pistol was out and pressed into his midriff. He grabbed the guy's arm and pulled him round so that he was in front of him. Quickly checking that they weren't being watched, he shoved him roughly in the back, pushing him forward.

'Just walk, nice and casual like. That's my boy. Now turn at this corner and walk along up here to my nice new police car.' He signalled for

Cassidy to lower the window. 'Hand me the keys,' he said. Taking the keys, he manoeuvred the guy to the back of the car. With his free hand he opened the trunk. Then he pistol-whipped the guy across the back of his head and he slumped forward and fell part way into it. Barclay put his arm under the guys legs and hoisted him all the way in.

Then Barclay leaned into the trunk, gripped the guy's head in his massive hands and twisted it sharply. Cassidy heard the sickening crack from inside the car. If he'd have eaten an evening meal it would have reappeared there and then. Instead he just felt the bile rise to his throat.

Barclay slammed the trunk, and holding the newly acquired two way radio he came back and got in the passenger seat.

'OK,' he said as casually as if he'd just returned from an evening stroll, 'Let's go, it's approaching midnight. They'll be coming out soon.'

Cassidy realised he'd missed his opportunity. The machine pistol was still on the seat. He glanced at it and then back at Barclay.

Barclay saw what Cassidy was looking at and

grinned at him maliciously. 'You haven't got the balls little man. But if you want to try reaching for it be my guest. But remember this, when you don't make it before me, I'll not only use it on you, but I'll also go to your house and use it on your ma as well. But not till after we've done what we're here for. So, think on that while you're driving back to where we were before.'

Cassidy shook his head resignedly and edged the car out of the side street.

The police officer who Barclay had killed was not missed by his colleagues in the bar because he was only supposed to radio in if he saw anything suspicious. In that respect no news was good news, and it worked out well for Barclay, who at approaching one in the morning, was still parked with Cassidy three blocks along from the bar in South Canal Street.

00.40 Friday 22nd September 1995. O'Halloran's Bar.

In the bar the revellers were saying their goodbyes. Many of them had to report for work the following morning and didn't want to overdo it. As they started to drift out of the door of the bar Barclay sat up straight. From the number of people coming out it looked like everyone was leaving together. He pulled out a small pair of binoculars. He scanned the crowd. He could see the front of the bar well enough, but it was difficult to make out the individuals, and he wanted to be sure. He held the binoculars in his left hand and kept his right on the machine pistol.

'Be ready Cassidy,' he said. 'On my word you drive to the bar and pull up opposite, and you don't drive away until I tell you.'

Cassidy didn't answer.

'Did you hear me Cassidy?' he yelled.

'Yeah, I hear you Barclay.'

'Well fucking answer me then.'

'Why, you're gonna kill me anyway, so what difference does it make?'

'I ain't got time for this shit now Cassidy. This is gonna go down any minute now,' Barclay said pointing towards the bar. 'So listen to me for the last time. You do this, then you, and your mother both live, I swear it. But if you don't, then you know what's going to happen.'

Barclay was starting to worry. It looked like everyone had gone, but there was no sign of his target. Could they have gone out of a rear entrance? Did they know he was there? Had the cop he'd killed managed to get word to them beforehand?

The thoughts had hardly formulated in his mind when he saw Mike walk out of the bar. He quickly raised the binoculars to make certain. Yes! It was Mike Riley, smiling broadly, arm in arm with a tall, elegant woman who he assumed was his wife. Barclay couldn't believe his luck, because behind Riley was Nathan Weiss. Nathan was talking to another guy who he thought he recognised from somewhere but couldn't place him. That other guy was actually Lionel. Behind Nathan and Lionel, busy chatting happily were Abbey and Rebecca, who had quickly bonded and were already very close. All six of them were in a tight group. Perfect!

'Go Cassidy, now!'

Reluctantly Cassidy powered the cruiser forward and pulled up sharply across the road from the O'Halloran's. Another stroke of luck for Barclay was that there was a fire hydrant on the sidewalk outside of the bar. Obstructing fire hydrants is prohibited so the kerbside was free of vehicles, which meant that he had a clear view. The few cops who were still in attendance keeping watch were standing off to the side and didn't take much notice. They mistakenly assumed that the officers in the vehicle were some of their colleagues who were tasked with the same objective. Keeping mike Riley safe. Because Barclay was so large he obscured their view and they couldn't see that the driver was little bigger than a child. Even when the passenger window lowered they still paid little attention. Until one of them saw the barrel of the machine pistol come through the window and point in their direction.

'GUN! DOWN!' he yelled, 'EVERYBODY GET DOWN!'

The Finnish Jatimatic automatic machine pistol

first caught Barclay's eye in the 1986 Stallone movie Cobra, and he immediately sought one out. He favoured it because it was as light and easy to use as a regular hand-gun, and it could carry an extra capacity magazine. Barclay had fifty 9 millimetre Luger shells loaded in it and readily available to fire at his unsuspecting victims. A spare mag sat on the seat next to him close to hand in case he needed it during the getaway. He started firing even before anyone had hit the deck.

The first to be hit were the two officers who upon spotting the danger had bravely moved to the front of the small crowd. They died instantly as each of them received two bullets to their upper torsos. The firing was so rapid that before they had even fallen Mike and Rita were hit and killed instantly. Lionel pulled Rebecca down at the same time as he dived to the floor in an effort to reach one of the police officer's weapons. He screamed as a bullet ripped through his shoulder. The same bullet went clean through and into Rebecca's neck as she was behind him. The bullet went into her jugular and the spray of crimson red blood jetted across the sidewalk and ran down the window of O'Halloran's bar, obliterating some of the letters in the gold signwriting. She bled out in a matter of seconds. Lionel had lost consciousness and so was unaware that his wife had died.

The noise from gunfire and the screaming alerted the few straggling guests who were still walking to their cars and they ran back, weapons raised to try to help, but they were confused. They didn't immediately realise that the assault was coming from the police car.

Barclay carried on firing. He reckoned he still had half of the magazine left but he hadn't hit Nathan, his other prime target yet. He noticed a pungent smell coming from next to him and realised that Cassidy had soiled his pants.

'Stay put Cassidy,' he shouted over his shoulder, 'we're nearly done here.'

Nathan, realising there was no cover, nothing to hide behind, and that they would be fully exposed if they tried to run was desperately trying to get himself and Abbey back into O'Halloran's. But the manager had locked the door after the last of the guests left. He kept

Abbey between himself and the door and he was banging on it when a bullet ripped into his spine. He groaned and fell in a heap to the floor. Abbey turned and screamed 'Nathan,' and was felled as another bullet ripped into her stomach. She dropped next to Nathan and passed out holding him and sobbing.

Barclay turned the pistol on the few officers who had rushed to assist and had now realised where the assault was coming from. They were kneeling in the street and firing at the cruiser. He emptied the magazine into the blue uniformed line of men and women, and they fell like nine-pins after a strike had been bowled.

The machine gun clicked. The magazine was empty.

'Drive Cassidy,' Barclay shouted, 'you know the route, back to Foreman's.'

Relieved that the firing had stopped Cassidy gunned the cruiser and the vehicle virtually left the tarmac as it surged forward. Barclay ejected the empty magazine and threw it onto the bench seat, grabbed the replacement and shoved it into place. He looked back and saw the strobe lights of two cruisers which had raced towards the scene of carnage. They had to slow and swerve around the bodies of the policemen and women which were strewn across the street. Another break for Barclay.

Driving expertly at high speed, Cassidy quickly approached the point where Foreman was waiting in the dumpster truck. Barclay leaned across and threw the switch for the vehicle's siren to kick in. They passed the truck and Cassidy pulled up sharply.

As arranged Foreman immediately manoeuvred the truck across the road and blocked it. Snatching the keys out of the ignition he jumped out and ran to the police cruiser, flung the rear door open and threw himself into the back seat. Cassidy shoved the car back into drive and raced away. The pursuing police cars screeched to a halt. They were stymied. The truck blocked the whole of the narrow road. There was no room to pass either side, and no side streets to reverse up to and divert around. Barclay had chosen the location well. Cassidy was clean away. Barclay hadn't even needed to use the second magazine.

Cassidy drove back to Foreman's. As they pulled up outside Foreman hurriedly opened the shutters and Cassidy drove in. Foreman closed the shutters. The workshop was in an industrial area which was deserted at that time of the morning so they had arrived totally unseen.

Cassidy and Barclay disembarked the cruiser.

'Howdit go?' Foreman asked Cassidy, turning his nose up at the fetid smell which had spread from the car and now engulfed the workshop.

All Cassidy would say in response was, 'you got somewhere I can clean up please Stan?' He wasn't embarrassed. He didn't care. All he wanted to do was go home and hug his mother. But he doubted that Barclay was going to let either him or Foreman leave alive. But he wanted to clean up. He felt disgusting, and hoped that if he stripped out of filthy clothes he was wearing, he could maybe wash away some of the awful scenes he had witnessed. *"Unlikely though,"* he thought, *"the memories of what I've just seen are going to haunt me for the rest of my life."*

'Sure, Lance,' Foreman said sympathetically. 'There's a shower stall at the back on the left, next to the toilet. Your own clothes are in a cupboard out there as well. I assumed you'd want them.'

00.57. Outside O'Halloran's Bar.

The paramedics pronounced Mike, Rita and Rebecca dead at the scene of the shooting. They worked feverishly on Lionel, Abbey and Nathan before rushing them away in ambulances to Chicago General, where teams were waiting for them at the A & E.

The whole area was sealed off as the forensic team scoured the area, collecting items and carefully placing them in plastic evidence bags. Several bullet casings were picked up. They especially searched the area where the cruiser from which Barclay was firing had been parked. After two hours they concluded that there was not much more that they could do and left.

Inside O'Halloran's, Les Curtis and John Saunders sat at a table conferring. Curtis's face was red. He had unashamedly cried. Not only was he devastated at the loss of his one-time boss, but he had also secretly had a crush on Rita for years, something that only John Saunders knew.

'John, it was Barclay. It had to be. Nathan is right. He ain't dead, he didn't fucking drown in

239

those docks, and now he's back. It was him who blew up the clinic and now he's slaughtered all of those innocent people right under our fucking noses.'

John squeezed his partner's and closest friends arm. 'We'll get him Les, if it's the last thing we do on this rotten earth. We'll get him. So where do you want to start?'

'We scour the map. A half-mile radius of where the dumpster truck blocked the road. They won't have risked driving the police car much further away than that. Which means they will have had to either dump it, torch it, or or hide it. If it's not on the street then it's in a lock up somewhere. We'll look in every single one until we find it.'

01.10. Stanley's Workshop.

Barclay and Cassidy were both dressed and ready to leave.

Barclay looked at his watch, pointed to the car and said to Foreman, 'Foreman, your first job, before you do anything else, is to strip out the modifications you made for Cassidy. Wait until four o'clock. That's the time when there's the least number of people about. Then take the car to the woods on the outskirts of the city and torch it.'

'How will I get back, will you or Lance follow and bring me?' Foreman asked.

'No, I'll be long gone and Cassidy will be lying low for a few days. Get a bus, wear a baseball cap Just keep your head down and avoid looking at any cameras. Come on Cassidy, let's go.'

'Hey Jake,' Foreman said.

'Yeah, what?'

'You mentioned something about ten grand.'

'It's in the glove compartment of the cruiser. Make sure you take it out before you torch it.'

Foreman laughed, 'sure Jake, thanks' he said.

From the look on Barclay's face he knew better than to check it in front of him. It   implied mistrust. And deciding that if there was an option between Jake leaving him alive, and the ten grand not being where he said it was, the former was the choice which he would more happily accept.

'You did well Cassidy,' Jake said to him as he drove them back to the motel, taking a circuitous route through the back streets to avoid the possibility of any road blocks.

'Did well?' Lance moaned. 'You mean while I was assisting you in a mass murder of all those innocent people? What did any of them ever do to you? And what's my reward going to be? Have you got ten grand for me as well, cos I don't want any blood money?'

'No Cassidy. Your reward is that your ma is going to live to a ripe old age. There's just one condition.'

'And what's that?' Lance asked cagily.'

'That I always know where you are. If you move you let me know. I'll check the classifieds in the Chicago Tribune on the first of every month. If there's an ad saying,' he thought for a moment, then grinned and said 'Lance your painful boils, with a post box number, any number, it doesn't have to be a genuine one, then I'll know to call you. So don't change your cell phone number either. Have we got a deal?'

'I guess,' Lance said quietly.

They pulled up at the back of Barclay's motel. Barclay disembarked and walked away without saying another word.

Cassidy drove back to his home, where he crept silently into his mother's room, laid on the bed next to her, gently draping an arm over her, and tried not to cry so that he wouldn't wake her up. The visions of the victim's bullet-riddled bodies being flung around with blood spurting from them in all directions haunted him. He squeezed his eyes closed trying to shut the awful pictures out of his head. Exhausted, he eventually drifted off to sleep. But every few minutes they persistently invaded his dreams and woke him up with a start. Concerned that he would disturb his mother, he gave up trying to sleep. He slid off the bed and quietly went to sit outside on the porch, where he wept while he gazed morosely at the stars, prayed to God for forgiveness and waited for the approaching daybreak.

Barclay waited for Lance to drive off, got in his Mustang and then drove back to Foreman's. The instructions he left with Foreman about the car were only to keep him from leaving the workshop. He had other plans for him. He had never liked him or trusted him. Ever since their days in Vietnam he had known that he would kill him one day. Foreman had grassed him up to his Captain, Mitchell Clark, after a foray into a civilian village, saying that Barclay had shot and killed innocent men, women and children. It was true of course, but Barclay denied it, saying that they were killed accidentally, claiming they were the collateral damage of warfare. It was Foreman's word against his. Barclay was the senior of the two men, and considered the better soldier, so Clark preferred to believe him. But since they had returned from the war Barclay had found Foreman useful over the years, so he had put off his inevitable fate. But now he had a second reason for killing him. He didn't trust him not to inform on him to the cops and do a deal with them to save his own skin.

An hour having left the workshop he was back

there and He tapped on the back door. Foreman opened it and Barclay barged in.

'Did you strip it out like I said?'

'Sure,' Foreman said, recovering from the shock of seeing Barclay again. 'I broke it all down and binned it. It was only a few only cables and some levers. It didn't take long.'

'And did you find the ten grand?' Barclay asked with a sick smile.

'No. I didn't expect to,' Foreman said.

'Clever man,' Barclay said. 'You know why I'm here don't you? I've owed you for all these years. Now it's payback time.'

Barclay remembered that the machine pistol was still in the police cruiser. His own handgun wasn't silenced, and a shot at that time of the morning might be heard by people living in the apartments above the neighbouring buildings. But he wasn't concerned. He didn't need the gun because he knew that Foreman didn't carry one. So he edged towards him, drawing his hunting knife from the sheath on his belt. Foreman reached to his workbench and picked up a long handled wrench. The two men circled around the pit where the cruiser sat on the ramp.

'I was half expecting this Barclay,' Foreman said. 'You ain't nothing but a murdering bastard. You don't give a shit about nobody, not unless they can do somethin' for you. And when you don't need 'em anymore you kill 'em, just like you're throwin' out some useless piece of trash. Well you ain't getting me without a fight.'

'Brave words Foreman. Well, you should know. You've been nothing but a useless piece of trash yourself for a long time. You've had it comin' ever since you snitched on me to Clark. I've just been too busy to get around to wasting you. But now, well, here I am and I ain't gonna take the chance that you won't rat me out to the cops just to save your own worthless skin.'

'I watched you kill those poor helpless peasants Barclay. I saw how you enjoyed pumping all those bullets into 'em. The look of fear on those kids' faces has haunted me ever since.'

'You poor stupid sap. Didn't you realise they would have told the Vietcong where we were? And I'll bet that to save your own ass you'll be just like them slitty eyed little fuckers and tell the cops where I am.'

The two men continued their deadly dance around the ramp, never taking their eyes off of one another.

'Nah, not them, Foreman said, they didn't like the Vietcong any more than we did. That was just your excuse. Just like it is now.'

'You can believe that if you like. But you still didn't have to go running to the captain did you? We were pals, comrades, fighting together and we were supposed to be watching each other's backs. Instead you tried to stab me in mine. So now, I'm going to gut you like a fish.'

'I was never your pal Barclay,' Foreman countered, edging back trying to stay out of reach, 'I've always hated you. You're just a cruel bastard and a bully. You make me want to vomit. And killing me ain't gonna solve nothing. You think the cops don't know it was you who gunned down those people at the bar?'

'Course they know it was me. But it ain't me I'm worried about you ratting out Foreman. I can take care of myself. It's Cassidy, cos he can't. And there ain't no way they can tie him up to it, unless you tell 'em.'

'You going soft Jake? Since when you ever worried about anybody else?' Foreman taunted.

'Believe it or not I like the man. One of the few people I ever have. He's a harmless little guy. And I frightened the shit out of him by threatenin' his ma to get him to come along tonight. Something I ain't proud of. So I ain't gonna let you fuck him up. I'm gonna fuck you up instead before you get the chance.'

Barclay moved in, crouching, rocking on the balls of his feet from side to side and making "come on" gestures with his free hand, encouraging Foreman to make a move. Foreman took the bait and swung the wrench with his right hand, but it didn't connect because Barclays massive left hand came up quickly and caught hold of Foreman's wrist, while his left plunged the hunting knife under his ribs, slicing into his heart killing him instantly. Foreman exhaled a last rasping breath and when Barclay withdrew the knife he collapsed in a heap onto the oil stained floor of the workshop.

Wasting no time Barclay grabbed the body and

threw it into the back of the police cruiser. He removed the machine pistol from the front seat and put it onto a workbench, making a mental note not to leave it behind again. In case Foreman had already spoken to the police, he checked the trunk to make sure that the body of the cop he'd killed earlier that night was still there. Good, it was. He left the trunk open.

He found a can of gas, opened it, soaked a rag with it, opened the cruiser's filler cap and stuffed the rag in, leaving most of it hanging down the side of the car. Then he backed up to the rear door of the workshop, pouring remaining the gas on the floor as he went, and picking up the machine pistol with his free hand.

Moving out of the door he lit a match and tossed it through the open doorway. The workshop was quickly engulfed in flames. He jumped back into the Mustang, started the engine, drove a little distance away, stopped and waited for a few seconds. He sped away as the police car exploded, taking the workshop with it.

He didn't go back to his motel room, there was

no point. He'd left nothing in there. Instead, satisfied with his evening's work he set out on the eight hundred mile journey to New York.

06.00 Friday 22nd September. Chicago General Hospital.

Various nurses and doctors attended the three patients. Lionel was the one of least concern. He was still unconscious, but his wound was a clean through bullet hole, with no damage to his major arteries and no bones broken. He would heal quickly. The attending doctor would tell him about Rebecca when he regained consciousness. Les Curtis had managed to find Miriam's number and contacted her to tell her about the tragic events of the previous night. She undertook the awful task of telling Lionel's children and moved them in with her and Eugene.

Nathan was under the care of an orthopaedic surgeon. The bullet had been removed, but it had shattered two of his lower vertebrae, L4 and L5. The surgeon had already speculated to his colleagues that it was unlikely Nathan would be able to walk again.

Abbey was the one who they fretted over the

most. She had been hit by two bullets. The first had hit her left lower leg and cleanly broken her tibia. That would mend quickly and was of little concern. But the chief obstetrician had a much more major issue to deal with, the like of which in his thirty years of practice he had never come across before. The second bullet had entered her womb and lodged into the chest of one of her babies. That baby's heart had stopped beating immediately. But the other baby was still strong, and appeared to have survived the trauma. Abbey had lost blood but had received a transfusion and the consensus was that she would fully recover. The decision which had to be made was what to do about her babies. The doctors were keeping her sedated for the time being. Abbey and Nathan were unaware of the problem they were going to have to face. But when they were both well enough they would have to be told, and together with the doctors would decide on a way forward. The chief obstetrician already knew what that would have to be. But he would still need their consent.

17.15 Friday 22nd September. Stanley's Workshop, Chicago.

The Fire Department were just about finished their preliminary investigation at Stanley's Workshop. There was little doubt that the cause was arson, and that the burned out police cruiser was the one taken from the two cops, Archibald and Blair, who had been found murdered earlier that morning at Fat Joes café, alongside the body of the owner Joe Catchpole. An emergency autopsy was ordered on the two bodies which had been found in the cruiser. The body in the boot had been identified as detective Milt Dickerson, who had gone missing the night of the 21st, before the shooting started. It was assumed that the body in the back of the car belonged to the workshop owner. Later, a DNA test would confirm it.

Les Curtis, who was still in bits over the loss of his friend, but had refused to go home stood talking to John Saunders.

'This is all Barclay's work,' he said. 'He took the cruiser early on Thursday morning. He must have holed it up in here till that night. Then used it on the shooting. The guy in the back must have been the driver. Barclay didn't want to leave anybody around who could finger him.'

'I get that Les,' Saunders agreed, 'but what about Milt?'

'Barclay must have spotted him casing the street and got the drop on him. No other explanation. What's another corpse to an animal like that?'

'There's just one thing I don't get though Les?'

"Yeah, what's that?'

'Who was the third guy?'

'What third guy?'

'Well, if this is the driver in the cruiser, who drove the dumpster truck? There had to have been a third guy.'

'You're right. I'd forgotten about the dumpster truck. The cops who were chasing Barclay said whoever was driving it got out and jumped into the cruiser. So this could be him, which means someone else was driving the cruiser. So we've got a missing accomplice.'

Saunders looked at the body of Milt Dickerson as it was wheeled away on the gurney towards the ambulance, and then he glanced back at Curtis.

'No,' Curtis said, 'I'm not having that, no way John! Why?'

'I don't know Les, but he conveniently disappeared from where he was supposed to be watching the bar and now he's turned up dead here with this other guy, who we are pretty certain must have been involved.'

'Look,' Les said, 'Barclay is our priority. Let's concentrate all our efforts on finding him. Maybe if we get lucky we'll also find whoever else was in on it. But right now I ain't prepared to believe that a young cop could have been involved in killing another cop. Why the hell would he be? And Riley was a good guy, you know that. Listen to me John. Dickerson's dead, so I'm gonna look into this as if he's another victim as well. We at least owe him and his family that until we find out otherwise. Agreed?'

'I suppose so Les. I just don't think we should dismiss any possibilities that's all.'

'Did we hear anything from Donaghy yet?' Les asked.

'Nothing as far as I'm aware. He disappeared from his beat, must be a few weeks ago now.'

'Well, Mike wasn't a big fan of his. He thought Donaghy was a fat lazy fuck who was on the take. And Donaghy knew it, so I think we should look into him as a possibility as well. Maybe he was driving dumpster truck. If we're going to be accusing a cop of being involved in this my money would be more on Donaghy that Milt Dickerson, that's for sure.'

'Ok Les,' John said. 'I'll get right onto it.'

The Fire Department chief came over . 'We're done here, for now anyway, Les. We've got everything we need.'

'Thanks Don, let me have your report as soon as you can. OK guys,' Les called out, 'seal it off now, let's call it a day.'

As they were walking back to their patrol car he looked at his watch. 6pm. 'John, drop me home please. I'm going to crash for two hours. At thirty six hours without a break, we're no good to anyone if we can't think straight. I suggest you do the same. Pick me up at 8.30?' We'll work through the night.'

'Sure thing Les.'

'Deeply immersed in their own thoughts they drove to Les Curtis's apartment block without speaking. John pulled up at the sidewalk outside. Les got out and banged his hand on the car roof to indicate his thanks and waved goodbye. He trudged up the steps to his front door, unlocked it, and hauled himself up two flights of stairs and let himself into his empty apartment. Empty, because his wife had walked out two years ago.

'First,' she screamed right into his face, when she was standing at their front door holding her suitcase, her lips drawn tightly over her teeth, 'you're never here. And second, I can't stand the way you always look all puppy-eyed at that Rita fucking Riley.' The door slammed behind her and he hadn't seen or heard from her since. Only from her lawyer and when the divorce papers arrived. He signed them and sent them back without a second thought.

He poured himself three fat fingers of whiskey and downed it in one gulp. Then without bothering to undress he collapsed onto the sofa where he fell into a deep sleep until John

Saunders rang the door-bell and woke him up
two hours later.

10.00 Saturday 23rd September. New York.

'Where do you want to meet?'

'Jake, you're here. That didn't take you long,' Krystal Brown said with an amused tone to her voice. During the day is too risky. Meet me for dinner. Do you know Brogan's Steak House in Manhattan? Its off the main beat so it'll be a bit safer.'

'I'll find it, what time?'

'Say, eight o'clock. And Jake?'

'Yeah, what?'

'After Thursday night's episode you're a real hot property. It's in every newspaper and all over the television. Every cop across The States is out looking for you. Make sure that you're not easily recognisable. And I don't mean just a stupid baseball cap.'

'I get it, what do you suggest.'

Krystal thought for a moment. 'Get yourself into a fancy dress shop,' she said.

'What? Are you kidding me?'

'No I'm not,' she protested. 'Listen long hair never goes out of fashion. Get yourself a long brown wig and a Mexican style moustache, and a casual shirt. Trust me, it'll lower the risk of your being recognised, I promise,' she said, trying hard not to laugh as she imagined what he would look like.'

'Yeah, and I'll look like a right fucking idiot.' he protested,

'Maybe you will, but an unrecognisable fucking idiot. I'll see you at eight tonight. Don't be late, I hate being kept waiting.' She disconnected.

Barclay, who was outside a drive-in MacDonald's smiled and hung up the phone. He grabbed the phone book, found and tore out the page for fancy dress shops. He pulled down the "stupid baseball cap" so that it almost covered his eyes. He got back into the Lincoln Continental which he had stolen in the early hours of the morning from a side street and which had on it the licence plates that he'd switched from a sedan he found parked a little further up the road. He set off to search for a fancy dress shop.

As he drove away he thought to himself, "How the hell does she know I'm wearing a stupid baseball cap?"

At eight sharp Krystal Brown glided into

Brogan's Steak House.

It was an ornately fitted out restaurant with a huge circular grill in the middle of the room where three chefs in white aprons were cooking enormous steaks and huge ribs on charcoal grills. The walls were bedecked in cowboy paraphernalia, saddles, leather chaps, hats, and massive steer's horns which were mounted on wooden blocks.

She looked around and it was all she could do to stop herself from letting out a scream of laughter. She drew a breath and held it to control herself.

Sitting in a corner booth at the back of the restaurant was Jake Barclay. He wore a large beige beaver stetson over a wig of long brown hair that came down to his shoulders. Under his hawk-like nose was a moustache which circumnavigated his mouth to fuse with a goatee beard. He wore a light tan leather jacket, navy denim jeans and glancing down she could see that he had on cowboy boots. He was staring down at the menu on the table in front of him. If he'd noticed her approach he didn't let on.

'Wow Jake!' she whispered as she sat down. 'You've gone the whole hog haven't you.'

'As they say, in for a penny,' Jake said without looking up, 'pointless otherwise.'

The truth was he had been excited at the thought of seeing Krystal again. He'd taken a shine to her years ago when she was a spirited kid. He'd followed her career, reading the articles about her in the newspapers, especially those which accused her of being on the wrong side of the law, admiring her progress and staring approvingly at the photographs of the stunning beauty which she had morphed into. Very few women had enthralled him over the years, but Krystal was certainly the one who had the most.

Although Krystal had given him a hard time on the phone, she had deliberately engineered the meeting for much the same reason. Jake Barclay, for all of his undisguised cold and cruel persona, had thrilled her to her boots the first time she met him. It was a feeling that she had never lost, or for that matter experienced with any other man, and she was eager to see him again. She didn't suspect that he had killed

Tyrone. Some of the cops she knew in the precinct had told her what happened. But because his body had never been found she did suspect that he wasn't dead. So she'd sent Earl and Jethro to Chicago on a pretence, and even when they reported to her what Donaghy had told them, she still pretended that was why she wanted to see him. Yes, she had a job for him as well, but the real truth was she had been searching for years for an excuse to meet him again. And now, here he was, sitting in front of her, and not only that, she also had the feeling that he had gone over the top with his disguise for her benefit.

Barclay looked up at the gorgeous face that he had only seen in newspapers for the past ten years. In the flesh there was no comparison. She was stunning, and he felt himself being hypnotised by her striking beauty. A feeling he had never experienced, and he struggled not to let it frighten him. Krystal sat down and they sat smiling at each other for ten or so seconds before he broke the silence.

Looking directly into the deep pools of her shining brown eyes he said, 'Krystal, I didn't kill

Tyrone. Yeah, I was pissed at him and in fact he was pissed at me when he found out what Kirkpatrick's real game-plan was. But I didn't kill him. Kirkpatrick did.'

'I know Jake, I never really thought that you did.'

Jake didn't know whether to laugh or be angry. 'So why drag me here Krystal?'

She reached across the table and gently placed her hand on his cheek. Jake flinched and Krystal quickly withdrew her hand. She looked hurt.

He looked away, embarrassed at his reaction, and troubled by the surge of feelings which he didn't think he was capable of experiencing. Up until this moment he had never liked to be touched by another human being. Other than when he had no choice because he'd been grappling with someone and fighting for his life. Or paying for sex. The last time he'd felt a hand on his face was when he was sixteen years old. His mother had slapped him because he didn't want to eat what she'd put in front of him for breakfast and he'd thrown it on the floor. He'd walked out of their home for good and his mother didn't see him again until his picture appeared on her television screen as the subject of a manhunt.

'I'm sorry Jake.' she said. 'I'm just happy to see you. We thought that you were dead.'

'It's fine Krystal. I'm just not used to being touched that's all. Not with any affection anyway.' He smiled sadly. The realisation of how he'd lived his life, and what he may have missed was slowly dawning on him. But he hated to show weakness to anyone, not even to Krystal.

Struggling to restore his tough persona he said, 'So, tell me, what do you need?'

'Well. There's a few things.'

'Well, maybe start with one, and if I'm happy to get involved with that, then we can move on to the others.'

She smiled. 'I assume you know I've a husband?'

'Yeah, number three I believe.'

She leaned forward and spoke in a whisper. The fragrance of her sweet perfume was intoxicating him, but he did his best to concentrate.

'Well, I need you to make me a widow again.'

She said it as casually as if she was asking him for a cigarette.'

'Why do you need me for that? You managed to get rid of the first two without my help.'

'The cops got a bit too suspicious after the last one. I was lucky with the first. He died of a heart attack. I knew he had a weak heart but I wouldn't let him get away without performing his connubial duties. He died right on top of me, so you could say I screwed him to death!' She giggled and looked at Barclay for a reaction. His face remained deadpan, so she continued. The second one suffered an anaphylactic reaction to a meal I made for him and he choked on his tongue. I mean, like I said to the cops, how was I to know he was allergic to eggs? He never told me.' She opened her eyes wide and stared innocently across the table.

Barclay remained silent, waiting for her to carry on.

'Jake, it's time for the truth, from both of us. I've been waiting for you for too long. And I think you like me too, am I right?'

The question caught him off guard. He nodded silently and they stared at each other. He was giving in. Jake Barclay, the hard man, the ruthless and heartless killer, had a weakness. And he was facing it in the form of Krystal Brown.

The waitress appeared. 'Are you two ready to order?'

They both broke off the stare, quickly picked up the menus and chose their meal. Jake went for a five hundred gram fillet with all the sides while Krystal opted for the ribs.

'How would you like your steaks cooked?' the waitress asked.

'Very rare and very red for me,' Barclay said. 'In fact why don't you just wipe its ass, cut the horns off and sick it on the plate?'

Krystal shrieked with laughter. 'What the hell has come over you Jake?'

'I dunno Krystal, it must be your influence I suppose.'

'Please excuse my friend.' Krystal said to the waitress, trying to stop herself from giggling. She hadn't felt this relaxed in a very long time.

'I'll have mine medium to well done please. And bring a bottle of your best Cabernet as well would you? Is that OK for you Jake?' she asked him.

'Fine,' he said.

The waitress smiled politely and thanked them. She said it would only take fifteen minutes and left them to continue their conversation.

'You know what I just did in Chicago, right?' Jake said.

'I know exactly what you are and what you've done Jake.' She lowered her voice to a barely audible undertone. 'It doesn't change anything. I ain't such an angel myself. That cargo ship that went up in flames and sank in New York Harbour three months ago. That was me, well with Earl and Jethro as well. It was sailing to Africa and I needed to add some of my own cargo. A shipment of pharmaceuticals. But the fucking captain didn't want to play ball. How was I to know that his wife and kids were on board, that he was taking them with, for like a holiday treat? They all died Jake, either burned or drowned, one or the other. But it was his fault Jake. He should have taken the fifty grand I offered him.'

'I guessed that was you,' Jake said. 'I know the police questioned you as well, but they had nothing on you. Look, this is a shit life. You get one crack at it, and you don't get given nothing. If you want it, you gotta take it. Nobody's out there giving you handouts. So don't go beating yourself up. You're right. If he'd had half a brain he'd have taken the fifty grand and they'd all be alive today. So getting back to business. How do you want me to deal with Aristos, that is his name isn't it?'

'I thought maybe a mugging gone wrong.' she said. 'Everybody knows he always walks about loaded with cash. I'll make sure I've got an alibi. We'll be at our regular private gambling club. He usually leaves before me. Especially if he's lost heavily and I'm on a roll.'

They stopped talking as a waiter brought their wine, and the waitress appeared with their meal.

When their drinks and food had been placed on the table and they were alone again, Barclay said, 'OK, let's just say I agree to do it. What then?'

'Well, I mentioned pharmaceuticals before,' she said 'That's the game now Jake. I've got sources. I import them and ship them straight back out on the black market, at a very nice premium. Some stay in The States and some to countries which otherwise wouldn't be able to get hold of them.'

'That's all very well, but where would I come in? What's in it for me?'

'I reckon I'll be getting enough once Aristos is dead and buried, so I thought a million bucks for you for starters.'

'A million bucks Krystal?' Jake interjected, doing his best to keep his voice down. 'Are you that desperate?'

'No, not at all,' Krystal quickly replied. 'Look upon it like a signing on bonus. I don't want to insult you or anything but business is business after all. Then after that we'll do it together Jake. You and me. Equal Partners. I'll pay Jethro off. He ain't smart enough for what I've got in mind. And anyway that man, he's a walking fucking time-bomb. The way he's carrying on, one of these days he's gonna get us all put in the fucking electric chair. I need to be well away from him. If Earl wants to stick around then I'll let him but he's going to have to toe the line and accept you as his boss. If he doesn't want to know I'll pay him off as well. Anyway, one of Aristos' properties is a lovely ranch just outside of Dallas, Texas. No-one's ever lived in it. There's a few hundreds of acres of land there. It'll make an ideal operational centre. We can build warehouses on it. I'll deal with the buying and selling of the pharmaceuticals and you can run the distribution. I'm sure you've got fake ID, and it's a perfect place for you to hide out in because nobody needs to know who you are. And we can get to know each other a bit better, if you know what I mean,' she said smiling seductively. 'What do you say?'

Barclay remained quiet for a few moments. He'd made his mind up long before Krystal had finished talking. And it wasn't only the million dollars Krystal was offering him either. Of course that helped, but more important was that this was his chance to quit the life he'd known. He'd hoped for an opportunity like this when he mistakenly thought he'd outwitted Kirkpatrick, but that had all gone shit-shaped. Getting out of the life now was majorly appealing to him, but the real clincher was the thought of being with Krystal, which was something that he could only have imagined.

He held out his hand. 'You got a picture of Aristos with you?'

'Sure.' she said, smiling. She fished into her purse, pulled out a photograph of her and her soon to be deceased third husband and handed it to him, holding on to his hand for a second or two as she did so. This time he didn't flinch. He didn't look at the photograph, he just stuffed it into an inside pocket of his jacket. Then she went back to her bag and withdrew a manilla envelope.

'What's this?' asked Jake.

'The keys and the address of the ranch in Dallas. It's registered to Aristos, but it'll be transferred to me with everything else when his estate is sorted out. And you know what, I doubt that he's ever set foot on it . Go straight there afterwards. I'll come and join you soon as it's safe for me to leave New York.'

Barclay considered briefly, and then nodded. He thought it was a good plan.

Krystal turned to the nearest waitress and held up her hand. The lights reflected of her bright red finger nails as she made the time honoured gesture of writing in thin air. 'Check please,' she mouthed.

When the check came Krystal tried to pay it but Barclay said, 'No. I'll get it. I reckon the next few days is going to set you back a million bucks.'

She didn't argue. They stepped outside into the fresh night air.

'Where to now?' he asked.

She pointed across the street to a Hyatt Hotel.

'Fancy getting properly reacquainted?' She asked. She didn't wait for a reply. Instead she hooked her arm into his and steered him over the road.

For the first time he could ever remember in a very long time, Barclay felt happiness in his heart and lightness in his step as he freely allowed Krystal to lead him.

Two hours later, an exhausted Barclay rolled onto his back struggling to get his breath back.

'Wow Jake,' Krystal giggled. 'You needed that all right didn't you honey? When was the last time?'

'Not that long ago,' he said.' But that was different. I was paying for it then and I just wanted to get it over and done with, put my pants back on and be on my way. You know, get back to wherever I was holed up and grab a shower.'

'And now?'

'Now, I ain't in so much of a hurry.'

Suddenly Krystal started giggling hysterically.

'What?' Barclay asked.

Krystal was laughing so much that she couldn't answer.

'What?' he said again, this time a little more firmly.

She crawled back on top of him. 'You've still got that fucking wig and moustache on,' she just about managed to splutter. She leaned her head down and kissed him, simultaneously gyrating her hips. Barclay groaned with a feeling of pleasure that he never thought he would ever experience and gave himself up to her all over again.

A while later, when they were both drifting in and out of a satisfied sleep, a sated Barclay broke the contented silence.

'Krys, if your plan is going to work I'm going to have to change my appearance, and I'm telling you now, surgery ain't a road I intend going down. I've heard too many stories of where that's gone wrong. I'm an ugly enough bastard. I don't need to risk making myself look worse by going under some quack's knife.'

'Hey, don't worry she said.' First of all you're not ugly, and second you don't have to. What's wrong with the disguise you're using now? Very few people would guess it's you.'

'Come on Krystal, I look like a complete idiot in this get up. I only did it because of you.'

'That's my point exactly. It couldn't look less like you. And anyway, I kinda like it.'

He thought for a moment. He was going to need a new photo ID.

23.30 Thursday 28th September 1995. The Flush, Manhattan

Krystal and Aristos were in their private club in downtown Manhattan. She was playing roulette. She was on a winning streak and was amassing piles of fifty dollar chips in front of her. Aristos, who'd lost heavily at blackjack, came over and laid his hand on her shoulder. He leaned his head forward and pecked her affectionately on the cheek. She glanced up into his piercing blue eyes and could immediately tell that the cards had fallen far less favourably for him than the little white ivory roulette ball had for her.

'I'm heading home sweetheart,' he said. 'Should I wait up?' he asked hopefully, the anticipation written all over his tanned face. He had grown accustomed to a good win for Krystal resulting in a good night for him.

'Sure honey,' Krystal lied. 'As soon as my luck looks like it's changing I'll be home. Don't worry I'll jump in a cab.'

Krystal knew of the fate which awaited Aristos, but couldn't see the point in bursting his bubble, so she let him leave the club knowing that he was looking forward to a session of lovemaking which was never going to materialise. He summoned his car from the doorman. He loved his maroon 1963 vintage Rolls Royce Silver Cloud with a passion and would not let anyone else drive it. Reluctantly he had to entrust it to hotel and club doormen, but he refused to employ a driver and only drove it himself. He slid onto the plush leather seats and set off towards his penthouse flat on Lennox Hill, overlooking Central Park on The Upper East Side. He steered the Rolls into the underground car park and guided it into the space reserved for the penthouse, which was situated conveniently adjacent to the private elevator and which would take him directly up to his apartment. Stepping out from the car he was immediately confronted by a large man wearing a black balaclava, and dressed in a leather jacket, jeans, black trainers and gloves. Barclay deliberately wore this outfit because Krystal had told him that there was a state of the art security camera and audio recorder pointed at the elevator. He'd agreed with her suggestion that it should appear to be a mugging, so he dressed for the part. Disabling the camera would have suggested too professional a hit. So Barclay stepped into full view brandishing a pistol and in a voice as different from his own as he could make it sound he drawled, 'Empty your pockets and give me your money man.'

Aristos hesitated. 'I don't have any money.'

Barclay bounced from foot to foot, and waved the gun around, as if he was agitated and drug addled. All part of the performance for the camera. 'You're a fucking liar,' he said. 'I know you got money. You don't get to drive a fucking car like that if you ain't got money. So give it to me before I blow your fucking brains out.'

Aristos still resisted. 'I've already told you, I don't have any money so why don't you go and try to score your drug money off someone else?'

Barclay couldn't have hoped for a more perfect response. Satisfied that enough footage had been recorded to convince anyone that this was a straightforward mugging, he shot Aristos twice in the chest. He stepped over to the fallen body and rifled roughly through Aristos's jacket and pants until he found his wallet, which he quickly shoved into the pocket of his jeans. He ripped off Aristos's Rolex watch and put it into his own jacket. Then he jogged to the other side of the car park, jumped astride the Harley Davidson which had been especially stolen for the purpose and exited up the ramp onto Lennox Hill with the hair of his long brown wig flowing behind him. He turned left into the underground car park of a department store four blocks down and parked the Harley next to a Chevrolet Impala, which Krystal had bought for cash from one of her contacts and parked there for him. He climbed into it and adjusted the seat back to accommodate his height and long legs. Making himself comfortable he drove out of the car park and headed out of New York towards the I-78 to begin the long drive to Albuquerque, before heading to Dallas.

11.00 Friday 29th September 1995. Albuquerque.

A week after the shooting in Chicago, Lance Cassidy was back at his desk in his office behind the repair shop. It was eleven o'clock in the morning and he was putting the finishing touches to a Gold American Express card for one of his regular clients.

He had the customary cigarette hanging from his mouth as he concentrated on his craft. Hearing a disturbance he glanced at his video security screen and watched as a large, long haired and bearded man whose face was partially hidden beneath a Stetson barged straight through from the front of the repair shop and banged on his door. He pressed the intercom.

'Can I help you please?'

'Let me in Lance.'

Cassidy felt his blood turn to ice. 'What do you want Barclay?'

'Let me in Cassidy. It's OK. I'm not here to make any trouble.'

Cassidy was confused. Barclay was speaking in a

tone that he wasn't used to hearing from him. It was docile, almost friendly. Reluctantly he stubbed out his cigarette into the ashtray which was jammed full of dog ends. Plumes of smoke eddied to meld into the fog which permanently swirled just below the yellowed ceiling above the office. He angrily slammed his hand down onto the door release. Barclay stomped into his office and plopped himself down into the chair facing him. He was actually smiling as if he'd come to visit an old friend. Lance felt his skin crawl and his stomach start to churn. It was only over the last few days that he'd started to feel a little better from the trauma he'd gone through on the night of the shooting.

'How you been doin'?' Barclay said.

Lance had prayed that he would never have to set eyes on Barclay again. And now here he was. In his office, facing him across the desk, taunting him. As frightened as Lance felt, he found it difficult to keep the bitterness from his voice.

'I'm sure you didn't come all the way here to ask about my health Jake. What do you need? And what's with the fancy get up? Why are you dressed like you're going to a rodeo? '

'Come on man, there's no need for that tone. Listen. I haven't come here to make no threats to you, or your ma.' He pointed to the photograph on the desk. 'How is she by the way? She's well I hope. I'm here because I want to completely disappear. If you help me and give me what I need today, I swear you'll never see me again.'

'What is this, some sort of an act? You think you can fool me by playing mister nice guy? I ain't interested. If I was to say no we both know that you *would* threaten me and my ma again. So tell me what you want and then you can be on your way.'

In all the years that he'd known Cassidy, Barclay had never been on the receiving end from him before. Cassidy had never had the balls to bad-mouth him. But he sort of understood, after all, he had put him through the mill that night. And Barclay needed what he had come for, so he didn't react. He just put some photo strips on the desk and said, 'make me some new IDs.'

An hour and two cups of coffee later the new documents were ready.

Cassidy handed them to Barclay. The new IDs were in the names of Ray Millington and William Unsworth.

'Here, this is for you,' Barclay said, dropping a fat envelope onto the table.

'What's this?' Cassidy asked suspiciously.

'It's a hundred grand. I figure I owe it to you for all the trouble I've caused you. Maybe you can take your ma on a trip or somethin''

Cassidy couldn't believe his ears. Fully expecting to be rewarded with a bullet between his eyes for his earlier outburst, he couldn't help himself.

Outraged, he shouted, 'what is it with you Barclay? You think you can virtually kidnap me, threaten to kill me and my mother unless I drive you around while I have to sit and watch you commit mass murder? I shat my fucking pants for Christ's sake! Then you waltz in here like my best pal and expect me to forgive and forget it all for a hundred grand?' He picked up the package and tossed it back across the desk. 'Please, just take your blood-money and go. You've got what you came here for. Now fuck off! Leave me the hell alone!'

Barclay nodded, smiled, picked up the package and walked out of the door.

'Be seeing you Lance,' he said as he closed it behind him.

'I hope not, I really fucking hope not,' Lance said. He watched his security screen to make sure that Barclay had left the repair shop. Then he stood, slid out the copies of all of Barclay's new ID documents which he'd made from under the folder where he'd surreptitiously placed them. He put them into the folder and locked it all away in his safe.

He lit another cigarette and took a deep drag. As he inhaled he started to cough violently, uncontrollably. He went to his cloakroom, grabbed some tissue and wiped his mouth. He looked into the tissue and saw thick blood red globules spreading across the fabric.

'Shit,' he said. 'That's all I fucking need.'

A half an hour later Barclay stopped at a roadside coffee house a few miles outside of Albuquerque and called Krystal on the throw away cell she'd purchased for them to communicate on.

'How did it go?' he asked her when she

answered.

'They interviewed me for three hours then they had to let me go. They suspect something,' she said. 'It's only to be expected I suppose. After all its not the first husband I'll be burying. I'm sure that they'll be watching me.'

'So what do you want to do?'

'You carry on to the ranch and get yourself settled in. Have a look around. Maybe spec it out for where we can build the warehouses. There's no food there but there's plenty of local joints that deliver take out. When the dust settles a bit here I can begin shutting things down, but that'll probably have to be put on hold for a while. It'll look a bit suspicious if I start on that right away. How about if we leave it this week and I come and see you next weekend?'

'Sounds good, but how will you do that if they're watching you? They might put a tail on you.'

'Honey, do you think that you are the only one capable of changing your appearance,' she said. 'How would you fancy me as a blonde, with maybe big round red rimmed glasses?' she added in a deep seductive voice. Trying to picture in his mind exactly what that would look like, and disappointed that he would have to wait more than a week to see it in the flesh, Barclay just said, 'OK. Let me know when you're on the way and disconnected the call.'

12.00 Thursday 28th September 1995. Chicago General Hospital.

Lionel was sitting in a chair in the private room shared by Abbey and Nathan. He had come to say goodbye because his wound was sufficiently healed and he had been discharged. He was preparing to fly home the next day to his children for Rebecca's funeral. A special flight had been laid on for him and for Rebecca, who would be in her coffin in the hold of the aircraft. Abbey and Nathan were both recovering slowly, and the day before had each received their horrifying prognoses from their doctors.

Even with the surgery and the aluminium cage they had fitted to support his lower spine, the orthopaedic surgeon told Nathan that the spine and nerve damage was so severe that he would never be able to walk again.

The obstetrician had told Abbey what he thought was the best course of action. She and Nathan were both devastated but he had explained that they had very little other option. For the sake of the baby who had survived she would have to go almost full term. Closer to her due date, when he considered it was safe to do so, he would perform a caesarean to remove both babies.

'The only thing I can say in consolation,' he said, 'is that the baby who has survived appears to be very healthy. Can I suggest you perhaps take the positive out of that, considering how much worse things could have turned out?'

In tears, they both nodded and reluctantly agreed.

All of the funerals took within a few days of each other. later. Mike and Rita were buried at the All Saints church in Chicago. Nearly five hundred people attended. About half of them were colleagues, past and present. The rest were family and friends. Les Curtis gave a moving eulogy, and although he tried to include some humour, he found it difficult. Looking down at the two coffins, laying side by side, with the photographs placed on top of them, especially Rita's with her radiant smile, he struggled to keep his emotions in check.

'Mike was a great boss and mentor. I owe my career to him. And when we were off duty he and his wife Rita were good friends,' he said. Although Les knew it wasn't the time or the place, he also knew that he would be forgiven for offering everyone who was assembled in the chapel the assurance that he would make it his personal business to find and apprehended the perpetrator of the heinous crime that robbed them of Rita and Mike Riley. He closed with the promise that he would not rest until he had brought them to justice.

At two o'clock on Sunday the first of October, at

the Bushey Jewish Cemetery in Hertfordshire, England, a similar number of people gathered to pay their respects to the family of Rebecca Streat. It was a typical early October afternoon. The weather was unable to decide whether or not to dispense with the cool autumn temperatures or let the winter colder climes take hold. The congregants stood around chatting respectably quietly while they waited for the service to start. The Rabbi spoke glowingly about Rebecca's life. He eulogised about her being a wonderful wife and mother to her three children. 'Yet,' he said, 'she still managed to find the time to carry out her communal and her charity work.' Lionel stood in the front of the crowd of men, with his arm across the shoulder of his son Solomon, who had his arm around his father's waist. It was difficult for onlookers to fathom which of them was comforting the other. Lionel looked across at his two older teenage daughters, Stella and Anita, standing on either side of Miriam, who was clutching them to her, being their rock. Tears flowed freely down their faces, and each time the Rabbi mentioned something that resonated with them, their sobs echoed around the chapel.

At nine o'clock on the Friday morning after the end of the shiva period Lionel phoned Nathan. It was two in the afternoon in Washington.

'How are you both?' he asked when Nathan answered.

'We're getting on OK I guess.' Nathan said. 'We came home from the hospital yesterday. Abbey's wound is healing. So is her leg. She's been advised to carry on pretty much as any other pregnant woman. Just to take it easy for a while till she's got all her strength back. She will, she's pretty resilient. The trouble is she's got me to worry about now as well. I'll never walk again as you know. A friend is taking us shopping for an electric wheelchair this afternoon. We'll try to make is as fun as possible, you know, look for one with go faster stripes and all the trimmings.' Nathan was trying to make it all sound as light as possible but Lionel could detect the hurt and irony in his voice. He was facing bringing up a child that he'd never be able to walk to school, to run around with, play baseball or soccer, or do the other things that dads who could walk do with their kids.

'How are you Lionel?' Nathan asked.

'I'm OK I suppose. Getting myself slowly back together,' Lionel said. Then he broached the subject that they had both been avoiding. The elephant in the room. Jake Barclay.

'I don't know is the truthful answer Lionel,' Nathan said, 'but I'm sure I would have heard if they got him. I haven't spoken to Les. I'm still on sick leave. He probably doesn't want to bother me. And I'm in the CIA remember so I should probably leave it to the Chicago PD anyway.'

'Will you be able to continue working Nathan?'

'Well I hope that I will. The doctor said I should be OK to go back to work if I want to in a couple of months. I'll be in a wheelchair but that won't be too much of an obstacle. As Assistant Director I was pretty much stuck behind a desk anyway. In fact Abbey and I had been discussing my going back out into the field. I don't suppose that will happen now though will it?' Nathan couldn't disguise the hurt in his tone. 'What about you Lionel? Have you got any plans?'

'As a matter of fact I have.'

'Really,' Nathan said, 'what are they?'

'I'm coming back to catch the bastard, Lionel said casually.'

'Are you serious?'

'As a heart attack.'

'How are you going to do that? Even assuming that the authorities here will allow you to get involved, what about your job, and your kids. They've just lost their mother Lionel. How do you think it will affect them? And anyway, they don't even know what your real job is. How will you explain it to them?'

'I've been thinking about it all week Nathan. I'm handing in my resignation. I've got twenty-five years with MI5. I can probably draw my pension. I'll get by. And I've decided that my kids are old enough now to know the truth. I kept it from them to stop them worrying, but they are all practically adults now. If I'm not honest with them now it will hurt them all the more when they do eventually find out. I spoke to Miriam and Eugene. Both of their kids are older, have married and moved out. They said ours, mine,' he paused, corrected himself. 'No ours, they will always be ours, they can stay with them.'

Nathan, empathising with Lionel's pain, said. 'When are you going to put all of these plans into motion?'

'I've got an appointment with my boss on Monday afternoon.' Lionel said.

'That's a coincidence,' said Nathan, 'so have I.'

'Good luck Nathan.' Lionel said, 'So maybe at the same time you can do something for me please?'

'Anything, what do you need?'

'Use your influence. Have a word with the Director. Ask him if he can help me to be seconded to work with Les Curtis at the Chicago PD.'

'And what if Les refuses, says that you're too close to it, too emotionally involved?'

'Tell him I'm coming anyway. And it's better if I'm working with him as part of his team rather than outside of it. He won't want a vigilante. Especially one as high profile as El Lion interfering with his investigation. And I might even still be able to draw on some of my MI5 resources.'

'You've really thought this through haven't you?' Nathan said.

'I've had plenty of time to think about it over the last seven days.'

'Leave it to me,' Nathan said. I'll do what can.'

'Thanks cousin,' Lionel said. 'I knew I could depend on you.' He hung up the phone and went into the lounge to speak to his children. To have the conversation which he should have had years ago, but had been putting off.

Their home was a large five bedroom detached house in Hillview Avenue. It was a location which they had deliberately chosen because it was nearby Sarah's home in Beethoven Gardens. It was tastefully decorated and furnished. Rebecca had always been careful to avoid anything which appeared ostentatious.

The children were sitting on the floor in the lounge playing Monopoly. They looked up at Lionel as he walked into the room. Solly, the youngest, was fifteen, Stella was seventeen and Anita, the oldest, was nineteen. Lionel and Rebecca had married when he was only twenty-two and she was just nineteen. Lionel wanted his children to be born while he and Rebecca were still young so as to avoid a large age-gap between them and their children. He had always felt that this was one of the major reasons for the problems which had existed between him and his father. Rebecca not only agreed to that but she also agreed to have all of their children as near to each other in age as possible to give them the best chance of being not only siblings but close friends as well. It had been tough in the early days, especially for Rebecca, but it had worked very successfully. Despite Lionel's regular and sometimes lengthy absences, a warm and loving harmony existed between the whole family.

'Hi dad,' Solly said.

'Hi kids, I need to speak to you.'

Lionel sat down on the sofa. The children turned to face him.

'How are you coping?' He knew it was a difficult if not a daft question to ask while everything was still so raw, but he felt that it had to be asked.

'Ok. I suppose,' said Solly. His face said otherwise. He was the most sensitive of the three.

Stella and Anita both nodded and smiled. They didn't answer. He realised that it was tougher for them. Losing a mother while so young is hard for any child, but for daughters, well, he couldn't even start to imagine.

'I've got a confession to make kids,' he started. 'I'm afraid that I've not been entirely honest with you.'

Anita said, 'dad, if you're going to tell us that you're a spy, then we already know.'

'What?' he spluttered, 'How? Did mum tell you?'

'No, she didn't have to.' Stella said, it was obvious. You didn't go from saving the Prime Minister's wife when you were about our age to becoming a boring civil servant. And anyway, most civil servants don't go flying off around the world every five minutes.'

'Especially those who've got like super-powers like you,' Solly added with a grin, referring to the amazing speed and strength which Lionel still displayed from time to time.

Anita said, 'when we asked mum, not all that long ago actually, she didn't deny it because she would never lie to us. But she asked us not to mention it to anyone else, and not to worry. She said that you'd always come home safe.'

That was more than Lionel could bear to hear. He started to cry. 'Yes, *I* did,' he sobbed. 'But she didn't.'

The three children moved to him as one and hugged him tightly. The four of them stayed in a huddle for a good few minutes. Then when his sisters went to sit on another sofa Solly stayed close to him.

'Listen,' Lionel said, 'I've got a very difficult question to ask you.'

None of the children spoke so he ventured quickly on.

'Would you mind staying with your Auntie Miriam and Uncle Eugene for a little while? I have to go away.'

'Where are you going daddy?' a frightened Stella said.

'It's obvious isn't it?' Anita said. 'You're going back to America aren't you dad? You're going after Barclay.'

Lionel wasn't surprised that Anita has sussed him out. She had always been the most astute and forthright of the three. Or that she knew Barclay's name. It had been all over the television news and in the press.

'Yes,' he said. 'I want to find the man who killed your mother and so many of my friends. But I'll be back as soon as I can. I promise.'

'But what if he finds you first?' Solly said. 'What then?'

'Solomon, I'm El Lion. He won't. So what do you say all of you? Will you give me your blessing to do this? For your mum, for my wife. I feel responsible. I owe it to her.'

'When would you go?' Stella sked.

'Next week, after I've told them at work on Monday. But that's assuming that my boss agrees, so at the moment it's only speculation. Then, a lot of the pieces of the jigsaw have got to fit into place first.'

Again, the three children moved as one into another family huddle and another crying session. Lionel had his answer, He was going back to Chicago.

Monday 8th October 1995. Whitehall.

At 4pm Lionel walked into the room where Commander Nigel Fletcher's receptionist was seated at her desk. She looked up and smiled warmly.

'How are you Agent Streat? I was very sorry to learn of your tragic loss. I'm sorry I couldn't attend the funeral. Somebody had to be here to man the portcullis and I'm afraid I drew the short straw.'

'Thank you Sheila. I appreciate the thought. I'm fine thank you. I've an appointment with the Commander.'

Sheila Strong wasn't just Fletcher's receptionist. A short and stout grey haired woman who was in her late fifties, she had been his right hand for as long as Lionel had known her. Nothing went on in that office that she didn't know about, but she was the epitome of the British secret service. Her middle name was "I don't know and even if I did I wouldn't be telling the likes of you!"

'He's expecting you. Go in please.'

Lionel knocked on the door and went in. Fletcher immediately rose from behind his desk, walked around it and extended his hand.

'My dear chap. How are you? Has your shoulder healed? Come take a seat. Would you like a drink?' He didn't wait for an answer. He went to the drinks cabinet and poured two healthy measures of 21 year old Macallan Malt Whisky into cut crystal glasses. He handed one to Lionel. Looking at his watch he said, 'Four pm. Well, I suppose the sun must be going down over the yardarm somewhere.' He chuckled and took a swig.

'Thank you sir.' Lionel said as he took the glass. He took a sip and passed a letter across to Fletcher.'

'Oh,' Fletcher said. 'Is this what I think it is?'

'I'm afraid so sir.'

Fletcher picked up his bone handled silver letter opener from his desk and slid it under the flap of the envelope. He cut it open across the top, with such deliberate precision, almost as if he was performing the most delicate surgery. He pulled out the letter and read it, then placed it on the desk. He smoothed it out with the palm of his hand before speaking.

'But why now Streat? Apart from the fact that you're still recovering from an injury, you're also still on compassionate leave. I'm not sure that I understand.'

'I take it that you are aware of how my wife died sir.'

'Yes of course I am,' Fletcher replied.

'Well, the murderer is still at large. He hasn't been apprehended yet. As far as I am aware, none of his accomplices have either.'

'So why does that mean you have to resign?'

'I'm going out there sir. I'm going to find him myself.'

'Why can't you leave it to the Americans? It happened in their damned country after all. Mind you. I've answered my own question really haven't I? I'm not sure you can leave anything to the Americans these days.'

Lionel ignored the comment. He stood up. 'Well sir, if that will be all, thank you for the drink.'

'No that will not be all Streat. Sit down please.'

Taken aback by the sudden change in Fletcher's tone Lionel sat back down.

'You don't have to resign.' Fletcher said, speaking a little more softly.

'How's that sir?'

'You have been with this agency for twenty-five years. You have guarded the life of three prime ministers and you've put your life at risk for this country more times than I care to think about. I am not prepared to let one of our best agents go off half-cocked to America of all places looking for some murderous scallywag. Do you even know where to start?'

As unhappy as he was at the circumstances that had brought him to this meeting, Lionel struggled to stifle a laugh.

'Has something amused you Streat?'

'Well actually, yes sir. You referring to Jake Barclay as a scallywag. It wasn't something I was expecting. I can't remember the last time I heard that expression. No offence sir, but it amused me that's all.'

'None taken. I'm pleased if I inadvertently managed to lighten the mood. So back to my question, and I'll put it another way. Where do you intend to start looking for the bastard?'

'Chicago sir. But it's more than two weeks now, the trail will have gone cold.'

'On your own?'

'No sir. My cousin, as you know is Deputy Director of the CIA . He's going to try to arrange for me to work with the Chicago PD.'

'He was shot as well as I understand it, wasn't he?'

'Yes sir, and his wife. He was crippled, but his intention is to continue.'

'Brave man. It must run in the family. Look Streat, I might appear to be an old fart to you, using words like scallywag and all that, but I'm a bit more worldly-wise than I'm given credit for. I have to be otherwise I couldn't hold on to this damn job. And to be honest I was half expecting you to waltz in here and say you wanted to go back out there to apprehend the man. I just wasn't expecting you to bloody resign. So, while you've been off I've run some interference of my own, behind the scenes so to speak. A British citizen was murdered, your poor wife of course, and you were shot as well, so I felt that I had the right. The FBI wanted to stick their nose in, which is their right as well. It's their job

305

in fact. But I pulled a few strings with some friends over there and persuaded them to hold back and leave it to the Chicago PD and the CIA, for the interim at least. After all, the CIA also suffered their own casualties.' Fletcher stopped for breath, studied Lionel's face for a second and continued. 'Streat, I have a suggestion. I'm prepared to stick my neck out and put you on extended paid leave. But you won't actually be on leave per se. Do you get my drift? You will have my and this agency's full support. For as long as it takes. Go and find this Barclay character and do what you have to do.'

'That's very generous of you sir, thank you. I don't know what to say.'

'You don't have to say anything. In this life Streat, you reap what you sow, and you've given enough to this country. But you keep in touch with me at all times to keep me updated. And if you need anything, you be sure to let me know.'

Then, Fletcher smiled, he picked up Lionel's letter, swivelled on his chair and fed it though the shredder, which made "whirring" noise as the sheet of paper disappeared though the rotating blades. He turned his chair back around and for the second time he extended his hand and Lionel shook it.

'*Now* you can go Streat. God speed.' Fletcher said, still smiling.

'Thank you sir.' Lionel stood and left the office a lot happier than he was when he had entered it.

All he had to do now was to tell his kids that it was no longer speculation. He was going back.

Nathan's conversation with the CIA Director didn't start off quite as smoothly as Lionel's had with Nigel Fletcher. The Director, Wayne Graham, was a fifty-seven year old brusque, reed thin six foot three sun-tanned and buzz-cut Louisiana born ex-marine. He had resented Nathan's swift elevation to Assistant Director, seeing it for what it was. A publicity cover up. But his power was insignificant against the real power-mongers in the White House, and he had to reluctantly accept that was what they wanted.

'I can still do a job sir,' Nathan said. 'And if I'm going to be paid a pension anyway, which I will, I'd like to be earning it.'

'Whether or not you'll be paid a pension is debatable Weiss, you weren't injured in service. It was on your own time.'

'Not exactly sir, Nathan said firmly. 'I was there in my capacity as a member of the CIA, as Mike Riley's guest. The Mike Riley who I helped to bring down your predecessor. The same Mike Riley who was murdered that night, with his wife, several other police officers, and one of my babies who was killed when my wife was also shot.'

Graham was stymied and he knew it. If he objected to Nathan's stipend he'd be vilified as a hard-nosed unsympathetic monster. In sporting terms he would lose the dressing room, the support of his team, and one can't run the CIA without it. Not only that, but he also recognised how popular Nathan was with his colleagues. They had never liked Kirkpatrick, The Director who Nathan had helped to topple. They had liked Barclay, his henchman, even less.

Nevertheless Graham still tried to put up an objection. 'Listen Weiss, Ironside was a TV programme. Raymond Burr was playing a part. That sort of thing can't happen in real life. You can't go out catching criminals in a wheelchair from a specially adapted van.'

'Sir, the Assistant Director doesn't do that anyway. You know that. He co-ordinates from an office. It's a desk job. And I didn't ask for my promotion, any more than you wanted me to have it. So, I have a suggestion, one which could work for both of us.

Graham hitched an eyebrow, 'Go on, I'm listening.'

'My dad really wanted me to be a lawyer. I was at law-school studying when my sister was killed. Her death was what caused him to lose his mind. My part in catching the gunman was what got me into the CIA. But my dad never knew that. He died thinking I was a lawyer. Anyway, I still carried on my studies. I passed all the exams I took and I reckon I can still finish the course part time and qualify, in two years max. Then I'll leave the CIA and take up the career in law my dad wanted me to have. I'll be out of your hair.'

Listening to Nathan's story, Graham finally softened. 'Listen, Weiss, Nathan, I respect your integrity. I know you didn't push for this job, more that it was pushed on you. But that doesn't mean that I have to like the fact that you have it. Or that I dislike you either. So yes, we have a deal. And more than that, I'll allow you any time off you need to complete your studies. On one condition.'

'What's that sir?'

'You get yourself into the DA's office and help put villains away. Not the public defender's office. They do the opposite and keep them on the streets. I won't help you do that.'

'That works for me sir. But I need Barclay to think he killed me. I can't have him knowing that he failed and coming after me and my family again. Can we have a publicity black out on the fact that I survived? It hasn't been mentioned so far.'

'And who do you think is responsible for that Nathan? I'm not the Director here for my good looks you know. Now, get yourself home and come back here when you feel up to it. Your office will be ready for you. I'll make all the arrangements for this place to be wheelchair friendly.'

'Thank you sir. I appreciate it, and I won't let you down.'

'I know you won't Nathan.'

05.30 Wednesday 10th October. 1995. Heathrow Airport.

Eugene pulled the crammed car up to Terminal Three. Next to him in the passenger seat was a contemplative Lionel. In the back were Anita, Stella and Solly. As miserable as they felt to be saying goodbye to their father, the children agreed before they left to give Lionel as cheerful a send-off as they could summon up.

'Look,' Anita had said. 'He doesn't want to go, to leave us all here. But he feels that he has to, that he owes it to mum. He feels responsible. He wants to put it right. So let's not make him feel any worse.'

They all clambered out of the car. Lionel and Eugene retrieved the luggage out of the boot and they walked into to the terminal to find the British Airways check in desk. When they got to it, Lionel turned around to his children. 'I'll phone every week, and be home regularly, I promise. Be good for Auntie Miriam OK?'

'We're not babies daddy,' Stella said.

'You don't have to be good for me,' Eugene quipped. 'I miss the fun of having my kids in the house. Make as much noise as you like. And don't worry about the mess. Auntie Mirrie will clear it up.' As usual, Eugene had managed to lighten the moment.

Lionel fished in his bag for his passport and ticket, and checked in his luggage. He had a final hug with each of his children in turn. After a solid handshake with Eugene and with teary eyes, he disappeared towards the diplomatic departure lounge.

Eugene and his new wards walked sadly back out to his car. All of them were crying quietly and holding on to each other for moral support. He walked slightly ahead of them to give them some privacy, only to find a warden planting a parking ticket under his windscreen wiper.

'Oi, hold on mate, I'm here, I'm going now,' he shouted.

'Sir', the warden said, his beady eyes and rimless glasses barely visible from beneath the peak of his cap, 'the sign clearly says no waiting or parking.' He pointed to the sign to reinforce his point. 'Drop off only.' he continued in his superior tone, 'and it's too late, I've written it now. If you want to you can make an appeal to the issuing authority.' The warden walked away in search of his next victim.

'Thanks pal, ' Eugene said, ripping the plastic bag out from under the wiper. He threw open the car door and stuffed it into the glove compartment.

'Unbelievable, fucking unbelievable,' he said. At the sound of hysterical giggling coming from behind him, he turned around to see Lionel's children who were standing behind him, laughing like drains. *Well if all it took to cheer them up was the cost of a parking ticket it was well worth it,"* he thought.

'Come on you lot, pile in, let's get you home.'

10.00 Wednesday 10th October 1995. Chicago O'Hare Airport.

Les Curtis was waiting for Lionel as he wheeled his bag through the special exit reserved for diplomatic visitors to the United States.

'It's very kind of you to pick me up Les,' Lionel said as they shook hands. 'I could have got a cab you know.'

'It's no problem Lionel, really,' Les said as they walked out to his car and got into it. It's good to see you. We're looking forward to having you working with us. Despite the rubbish they put in the movies, we welcome inter-departmental help. Especially when it comes to searching for an asshole like Barclay.' He edged out into the traffic and on to the Kennedy Expressway to head into the city.

'No progress then,' Lionel said.

'No, he's disappeared,' Curtis answered. 'We've got absolutely nowhere. All the case notes are on the desk we've set up for you at the station. It's next to mine and Saunders's. We'll go through everything with you as soon as you've settled in. Where are you staying?'

'I don't know, I haven't fixed anything up yet. I'm going to look for a cheap hotel room or maybe something in a boarding house.'

'Nonsense, you'll stay at my place. I've got room, as long as you don't mind the mess. Single guy and all that.'

'I couldn't do that Les. I don't want to put you out.'

'Hey, Lionel, tell me something willya. You've been seconded to me, correct?'

'Yes.'

'That means you have to do what I tell you! And I'm fucking telling you that you're staying at mine Have you got that clear, Mister El Lion?'

Lionel laughed. 'Yes sir.'

'Good, that's one thing settled then. Let's hope that everything else is as easy as that. We'll drop your stuff off and then get straight on to the station, or do you need a rest first?'

'No, it's fine. I grabbed some sleep on the plane.'

Twenty minutes later they walked into the squad room. Lionel was introduced to the team, who welcomed him warmly, offered their condolences and then left him to go and sit at his new desk with Les and John.

'What we have here is a long list of victims,' John said handing Lionel the top piece of A4 notepaper from the folder, which had all of the deceased's names on it.

Lionel scanned the list, and winced noticeably when he saw the name of Rebecca Streat, three down from the top, written beneath those of Mike and Rita Riley.

Saunders looked at Lionel sympathetically. 'Are you sure you're OK to go on with this?'

Lionel nodded. Next was a pile of photographs. Around twenty of them were of the scene outside O'Halloran's bar, showing the bullet-ridden bodies of the deceased before they were removed by the paramedics. Lionel averted his eyes when he saw what was clearly a photograph of Rebecca's body, lying bloodied with her arm resting against the bar door. Several were shots of the burned out cruiser in the fire ravaged workshop, taken from different angles . One was of what was once the back seat, with the charred corpse of Stanley Foreman sprawled across it. Another was of the trunk, with what was left of the young cop Milt Dickerson's body.

'You reckon this is also Barclay's work?' Lionel asked.

'No question,' Les said. 'Milt was on duty outside the bar, keeping an eye out for Barclay. But he disappeared. Then he turned up in the trunk of the cruiser they used on the job. Too much of a coincidence.'

'We haven't ruled out the possibility that he was involved somehow,' Saunders said.

'But we haven't ruled it in either.' Les said, throwing his partner a look.

'And this is all we have?' Lionel asked.

'I'm afraid so,' Les said. 'Barclay's in the wind. Until he shows himself again, we're chasing shadows.'

'What about known associates?' Lionel said.

'Up until maybe four months ago he was CIA,' John Saunders said 'Outside of the agency he didn't have too many. The one we knew about was Tyrone Saint Brown, and he's dead.'

'What about the driver. If Barclay was doing the shooting, what have you got on the driver? And who drove the dumpster truck?'

'Nothing,' Les said. 'Zilch. John here wants to look into Milt Dickerson for that, but I disagree. Clearly Stanley Foreman was involved. But we don't know how yet. Did he drive the dumpster or the cruiser? We're also looking into the possibility that it could have been .8ia missing cop called Donaghy s well.'

Suddenly Lionel was tired. The long day's travelling had caught up with him. Les could see him struggling.

'You look bushed,' he said. 'I'll tell ya what, why don't we all get a drink, then call it a night and attack it refreshed in the morning?'

'I'm seconded to you,' Lionel said. 'So you're giving the orders. Lead the way.'

Six fruitless months had passed. It was as if Barclay had been plucked from the face of the earth by Martians, and Lionel, Les and John had just about exhausted every avenue of enquiry.

Lionel reported regularly to Fletcher, and went to see him once or twice when on his monthly visits home to see his family. His children were always excited to see him and looked forward to the opportunity to spend the weekend with him in their own home. After a few visits they became used to the fact that he had to return, and gave up asking how much longer he would have to spend away. They accepted the fact that he was on a mission, one which he was determined not to give up until he had completed it successfully. But what they couldn't see was that their father's resolve was weakening. As much as Lionel wanted to exact retribution on Barclay, he realised that he was missing his children far too much, and that being with them every day was more important. The wrench of leaving them after every trip home was tearing him apart. Rebecca would understand, even support him if he gave up, he thought.

As he ate his breakfast on the flight back to Chicago he decided to tell Les that this would be the last time he would be coming out.

3pm Friday 26th April 1996. Chicago Police Headquarters

The telephone on Les Curtis's desk rang. He picked up the handset and in a bored voice he said.

'Chicago PD.'

'I know how to find Jake Barclay.'

Suddenly alert, Les said urgently, 'Who is this?'

'Who I am isn't important. Do you want to know or not?'

'Hold on, I'll get someone to talk to you.' Les held his hand over the mouthpiece. 'Hey Lionel,' he called. 'I think you should take this. There's a guy on the phone says he knows how to find Barclay.'

Lionel grabbed the extension.

'This is Lionel Streat. Who am I talking to please?'

'Someone who has the information you need.'

'How do I know you're not wasting my time? Just like all the other hoax callers have over the last six or so months.'

'Please, just, listen to me. I saw what happened outside that bar. The people he gunned down, and it's haunted me over those same months. I want to do what I can to make it right. I know I can't bring those people back. But if I can help put Barclay where he belongs, it'll ease my conscience a little bit.' The guy's voice cracked a bit and he wheezed as he tried to catch his breath.

'Why are you coming forward now? Why all of a sudden is it bothering your conscience?'

'Because I was the one in the car with him. And because I believe that God pays debts, I'm dying myself now. I'll be dead within weeks. So I want to make peace with my maker. And the only way I can think to do that is to tell you what I know. So if you're interested, meet me in Clancey's Bar in 30 minutes. I'll be sitting in a booth at the back. You won't have any trouble recognising me. I'll probably be the only dwarf in the place.' Lionel was left listening to the ringing tone. He grabbed his jacket from the back of the chair.

'I'm going out,' he called as he stood up.

'You want me to come with you?' Les Curtis called out after him.

'No thanks Les, I'll be fine, I've got this,' Lionel

replied as he strode out of the office.

Lance Cassidy stood on tip toes to hang up the phone. He reached and grabbed his trolley with the oxygen canister on it and stepped away from the call box. He breathed a heavy sigh, relieved that he had made the call. Suddenly, he started having a coughing fit. He pulled out a handkerchief and held it over his mouth. The fit lasted for around thirty seconds. It was exhausting and it was all he could do to remain standing on his feet. He stepped back to the phone booth and held on to it for support. A passer-by stopped and offered assistance which he declined with a quick shake of his head. When the fit had subsided he looked into the handkerchief and seeing the blood splatters he shook his head sadly. He balled up the handkerchief, threw it into a nearby refuse bin and hailed a cab. As it drove up he pulled the trolley up to the cab, lifted it in with a struggle, laid it on the back seat, and fell into the cab next to it. He held the oxygen mask over his face, took a few deep breaths to regain his composure and gave the driver the address to Clancey's bar.

A half an hour later Lionel walked into Clancey's Bar and immediately spotted Cassidy sitting at the back. The oxygen canister was on the seat next to him. Lionel sat down facing him.

A waitress came over. Lionel pointed to the beer in front of Cassidy and ordered the same.

'So,' he said, 'why now, this long after the event? What are you after, a deal?'

'I'm not after anything, I told you, I'm dying. My deal is with a far greater power than you. I don't want to take what I know to the grave with me.' He slid one of the folders that were on the table in front of him towards Lionel.

'What's this?' Lionel asked.

'In case you think I'm bullshitting you. That's my medical records.'

'I'll decide if I think you're bullshitting me when I've heard what you've got to say.' Lionel said. He glanced down at the folder and saw the name on the front cover.

'So, Mister Cassidy, tell me what you know about that night.'

Cassidy coughed heavily, grabbed a napkin from the table and wiped his mouth. His eyes were watering from the effort. Looking directly at

Lionel he said, 'Jake Barclay, you know him, right?'

Lionel nodded.

'Well, he called me up and told me he wanted me to help him with something. I said I didn't want to get involved but he said if I didn't help him he would murder me and my mother. Just like that, he'd murder my mother. I had no idea what he had in mind, but I guessed he couldn't be up to any good. Plus I knew he was a psycho, and if he said he would murder my mother, then I also knew that he would. So I had no other choice did I?'

He paused, put his mask against his face and took a few deep breaths.

The waitress brought Lionel's beer, looked sympathetically at Cassidy and put it on the table. Lionel thanked her, took a sip.

Lionel waited for her to be a safe distance away before saying, 'you could have called the police.'

 'Nah, I was up to no good myself. That's how he knew me. And anyway, there was no guarantee they would have caught him, which wouldn't have helped me or my mother much would it?'

'They could have protected her, put officers with her around the clock.'

Cassidy snorted derisively. 'Man, you know who we're talking about here? This guy's ex-CIA, a psychopath and a trained killer. He's been dodging the police for years. Do you think a few raw street cops would have kept my ma safe? No way in hell. Not that it matters now. She passed last month.' He took a few more breaths of his oxygen. His beer still sat in front of him, untouched.

Lionel nodded to concede the point. ' I'm sorry, so go on please, when you're ready.'

'He told me to pick him up from a motel outside of the city and drive to a lock up in town. When we got there he had a Chicago PD car waiting inside which he wanted me to drive. He had two cop's uniforms for us to wear. He put one on and told me to put on the other one. Then I had to drive into the city and park down the road from a bar where some retired cop was having a party. He was waiting for the party to finish. He spotted a cop who he thought was on the look-out for him. He killed him and dumped his body in the trunk. Then he watched the bar again until people started coming out. He was obviously looking for someone in particular. Then he spotted them and he yelled at me to hit the gas, but slow down once we got outside.'

By now Cassidy was struggling to breathe. He stopped and put his face into the mask, and inhaled as deeply as he could. About ten seconds later he'd recovered enough to continue.

'The next thing I know he's mowed them down with a fucking machine gun. He screamed at me not to drive off until he'd finished shooting. It was carnage, fucking bodies everywhere, men women, policemen. The poor bastards didn't know what had hit them. They didn't stand a chance'.

Cassidy stopped again to take a breath and when he looked up at Lionel, he saw that his eyes were glistening from tears which had welled up.

'What?' He asked. 'Why are you crying?'

'Because,' Lionel said bitterly, 'one of the people you helped Barclay murder was my wife.

The policeman whose party it was died alongside his wife. His wife died as well. My cousin was crippled for life and his pregnant wife survived, but one of the twins she was carrying didn't make it. She had to go full term carrying a dead baby inside her. That's why I'm crying Mister Cassidy.'

Cassidy's face blanched. 'My God,' he said. 'I'm so terribly sorry, I had no idea. But what could I do? He had me between a rock and a hard place.'

Lionel didn't respond immediately. Instead he sat there for a moment recalling the awful and tragic moments when Barclay opened fire. Miraculously he had only been wounded and escaped serious injury. But the same couldn't be said for Rebecca, Mike, Rita, and the others who were mown down. Yes, Abbey had survived, but at what cost?

'Well,' he said grimly, 'I suppose you're right. It's true what they say. God pays debts, and it looks very much like yours is about to be settled, in full. So, if you tell me everything, and I mean everything, then maybe we can call in Barclay's debt too, because it's very overdue.'

Cassidy nodded sadly and slid the other folder to him.

'What's this?' Lionel asked.

'It's the latest IDs I did for him. He came to my office a week after the shooting. I couldn't believe it. He said he needed new documents and I was too shit-scared to say no. He turned up in some ridiculous get up and I did them for him. He tried to give me a hundred grand, but I refused it. I didn't want his fucking blood money. I just wanted him out of my life. Thankfully, that was the last time I saw or heard from him. So, in there is everything you need to know to track him down. Details of his fake passports, drivers licences, bank accounts. If he's renting a place to live, or even bought one, or maybe hired a car, he might have used one of those IDs or bank cards to get it.'

'So this is how you make your living is it, counterfeit documents?'

'Yes?'

'And you're happy for me to hold onto these, even though it clearly incriminates you?'

'Yes,' Cassidy said again. 'I couldn't care less now, what difference will it make. I'm on death row already.'

'And what do you want in return?'

'My cell number is written on the inside cover of that file. All I want you to do is to let me know that you've got him. If he ends up being killed, then that's absolutely fine with me. He's had it coming for a long time. And then I can die in peace. It won't wipe my conscience clean, but at least I'll be able to go to my grave knowing that I finally did something right.'

Lionel sat for a while in silence, pondering what to do.

'I'll be in touch,' he said. Then he stood, dropped a ten dollar bill on the table, picked up the folder and walked out of the bar.

He rushed into a nearby arcade, found a phone booth and called Nathan.

'We've finally got a break,' he said excitedly as soon as Nathan picked up.

'Slow down Lionel. Tell me. What's happened.'

Lionel pulled a photocopy of one of the passports out of the folder.

'A guy called, he said he knows how to find Barclay. So I went to meet him, and guess what, he makes false IDs.'

'Yeah, so?' Nathan said.

'For Jake Barclay. And I've got copies of them here.'

'Great, put an alert out. As soon as he uses one of them you've got him.'

'No Nathan,' Lionel said, 'I don't want to do it from the squad room. I want to keep it low key, under the radar.'

'Why.'

'Because I want to go alone. If Chicago PD finds out where he is they'll go down there mob handed. It'll just be another blood-bath. I can get him on my own I know I can, and I want to, for Rebecca.'

'I understand what you are saying, and why. But I just think it's very risky.'

'I'll be careful. I'll find where he is and stake it out. I'll take my time.'

'So, how do you suggest we play this?' he said.

'I'll go to an internet place now and fax you a copy of the IDs. Let me know when you get an alert. I'll take care of the rest.'

'Hold on Lionel, I'm dead, remember?'

'Officially yes, but the Director knows the score. He'll back you. Forward the copy to him and I'm sure he'll set up the alert.'

'I don't like it Lionel, I really don't. I don't get why you can't let Les and his boys handle it. It's not like they don't have the experience.'

'Nathan,' Lionel said, 'you forget. I've taken down some real heavies over the years. Barclay is just another one. Another bully. And I've been waiting the best part of seven months for this opportunity. Anyway, who knows how much longer it will be before we get a hit on his ID? When we do, I don't want to just be there as an official observer. That's all Les said I would be from the off. No, I want to be standing right in front of him looking straight into his eyes. I want him to know who I am and why. For Rebecca, for your baby, for Mike and for all the others.'

'Lionel, that makes it a revenge killing. It would mean that you are no better than him. Is that what you want?'

'Listen to me Nathan, please, I'm not going to just waltz in and shoot him. I'll give him every opportunity to surrender. If he doesn't, that will be his choice not mine.'

Nathan could tell from Lionel's tone that there

was no point in arguing. 'You must promise me that Lionel. That way I'll be able to back you if you do end up having to kill him and any shit hits the fan.'

'I give you my word,' Lionel said earnestly, which was good enough for Nathan. 'OK.' He said. 'Then this is what you do.

You go back to the station now and tell Les that the guy was a fruitcake. That you've had enough, you're giving up and going home. Then come and stay with me, off the grid. As soon as we find out where Barclay is you go from my place to do what you've got to do. Then when it's over, you go home.'

'You won't regret it Nathan.'

'If anything happens to you I will.'

'But it won't. So don't worry. OK if I get to you what, the day after tomorrow?'

'Yes, that will be good. You'll be able to meet my new son and your new second cousin.'

'What? When?'

'A month ago,' Nathan said, laughing.

'Shit, I mean, Mazeltov! I was so tied up with everything I forgot to ask you. I'm so sorry, please forgive me. How's Abbey? How did everything go?'

'And I should have called you to tell you, I'm also sorry, but things have been hectic here. It was a bit nerve wracking. She went into labour a week earlier than expected. They rushed her into the hospital, and she had an emergency Caesarean. They took one baby away, as we always knew they were going to, but thank heaven Abbey's fine and coming home tomorrow with a very healthy little boy.'

'Then the last thing you need is me under your feet with a new baby and Abbey recuperating.'

'No Lionel, that's exactly what I need . The nanny can't get here for a few more days, so your visit couldn't come at a better time. I hope you can remember how to change a shitty nappy!'

'I can, and it will be my pleasure, Nathan.'

2pm Monday 29th April 1996. Dallas, Texas.

Barclay had spent the previous weekend either in bed with Krystal or wandering around the ranch with her discussing where to put the warehouses and other outbuildings. The police had apparently given up on her for Aristos's murder, so it was safe to start closing down the New York operation. They had decided on a schedule and Krystal had gone back to New York earlier that morning.

As good as her word, over the last seven months Krystal arrived most weekends in a short blonde wig, huge red rimmed glasses and she always looked stunning. He was always happy and relaxed in her company. But now he was alone again. It was only Monday and already he was feeling lonely and missing her. It was approaching two o'clock in the afternoon and he was famished. He reached for his cell-phone and called the Italian restaurant which was in a mall just a few miles up the road.

'Gino's, can I help you?'

'Yeah, it's Ray Millington. Send me my usual pizza please. Put it on my card.'

'Certainly sir.'

'How long?'

'Fifteen minutes. Will that be OK sir.'

'No that won't be OK,' he snapped back. 'I'm starved. Make it sooner, and make sure it's hot.'

'Yes sir, will, there be anything else?'

But Barclay had already hung up and the guy in the restaurant was talking to himself.

Before put the order through to the kitchen he scribbled a note on the bottom of the slip, "con catarro in piu per il fottuto maiale americano." Meaning "with extra phlegm for the fucking American pig!"

The pizza arrived and while Barclay was enjoying the last slice Nathan's phone rang. It was Wayne Graham, the Director of the CIA.

'Nathan, I've got some great news. We've had not one, but two hits on the card. About an hour ago Barclay ordered a pizza to be delivered to a ranch in Dallas. And earlier today he paid a bill by phone for a local cleaning company. I'm faxing you the address of the ranch.'

'Can you also let me have the details of the

cleaning company please?'

'Thank you sir, I appreciate it.' Nathan waited for the fax machine to start buzzing and the message to appear. As soon as the two pages came through he grabbed the pieces of paper and propelled the wheelchair out to the patio where Lionel was sitting. Smiling, he waved them under his nose.

Lionel sat up straight and snatched them from him. He studied them before saying, 'Dallas. How long will that take me to drive?'

'Two days straight, or you can fly direct to Fort Worth. Pick up a car at the airport when you arrive. Best to do it that way, Lionel. You'll be fresher when you get there.'

'I suppose. I'll call the airport now and book a flight for the morning.How interesting, he orders take out and he has a cleaner. That suggests to me that he might live alone. I'll pay a visit to the cleaning company when I get to Dallas and find out what the cleaner's schedule is.' He looked at Nathan and smiled. As Hannibal Smith used to say, "I love it when a plan comes together."

22.00 Friday 3rd May 1996. Dallas, Texas.

The late evening sun was concluding its descent from the cloudless Dallas sky and disappearing behind the distant horizon. The sun's reflection faded from the white gloss timber clad ranch house walls. Apart from the occasional distant howl of a coyote, it was eerily quiet. Although it was a two hundred and fifty acre spread, it was small by Texas standards, but big enough and remote enough for him to hide himself in. Barclay kept himself to himself, eating many of his meals alone in different diners, some as far as ten miles away. Sometimes he had a take-out delivered. He didn't know it yet, but the pizza he'd ordered the week before was going to be the cause of his downfall.

Apart from a few horses in the stable across from the ranch house, he kept no other livestock. He had no ranch hands or help. He kept himself fit by mucking out the stable himself. He had no family to speak of. Nobody ever visited. That was apart from Krystal, the only person he had ever loved, who came from New York to stay over at the weekends.

An agency cleaner called twice a week, because housework was the one thing he refused to do. He didn't mind shovelling horse-shit, but clean his own toilet? No way!

It was 10 o'clock on Friday evening. The cleaner was due to call. Barclay restricted the cleaner to non-daylight hours. When the agency queried, it he told them to take it or leave it. They took it, and he paid the extra out of hours rate for the privilege.

He watched from a front window as the van pulled up in the fading light outside the house. The cleaner got out and went around to the back of the van and opened the rear doors, supposedly to offload the cleaning gear.

Alarm bells started to ring in Barclay's head. It was still light enough for him to see that it wasn't the short, stocky, middle aged black guy who was his usual cleaner. This was a lean and clean cut looking white guy, maybe a little younger. The cleaner, who was wearing latex gloves, closed the van doors and approached the house, holding a bucket in his left hand, casually swinging it by the handle.

Barclay stood by the open screen door waiting

for him to come up to the house. He offered no greeting.

Instead, he barked, 'where's my usual cleaner?'

'Good evening sir. I am afraid that your usual cleaner isn't available today.'

'Strange, the agency normally calls when he can't make it.'

'The agency doesn't know.'

'What the hell do you mean, the agency doesn't know?'

'Do you have a problem understanding English, ... Jake?'

Jake Barclay froze. Since he had lived there, no-one knew his real identity and he was still using one of his false IDs.

With his right hand he reached around behind him for the Glock nine millimetre, which not having been able to kick the habit, he still carried in his belt. But lack of practice had eroded his speed and he wasn't nearly fast enough. In one swift and smooth movement, before Barclay even had his hand on the grip of the gun, the cleaner had reached into the bucket with his right hand, pulled out a suppressed Beretta and pointed it at him.

Barclay slowly brought his empty hand back and dropped it to his side. Even though he realised he was a fraction slower than he had been when he was in his prime, he'd never witnessed anyone move so quickly before.

'Who the fuck are you?' he said.

'I'll give you some clues.' The cleaner said.

Barclay raised an eyebrow a notch.

'You murdered my wife.'

Nothing registered on Barclay's face. Only a cold hard stare.

'No? Well, here are some more facts for you. I'm sure that you remember when you shot and killed my cousin Leah Weiss in a synagogue? Well my name is Lionel, Lionel Streat. Six months ago I was outside the bar in Chicago, when you shot me and crippled Leah's brother, oh, and yours for that matter, Nathan Weiss, who you knew as Dean West. That was also when you shot his wife Abbey and murdered one of their unborn babies, killed Mike Riley and his wife, and several others who were there, who were just innocent bystanders. That was you, wasn't it Jake, who killed all those people in Chicago?'

Only one thing that Lionel had said seemed to register any reaction from Barclay, the mention of the name Dean West.

'West? Only crippled? He's not dead?'

'No, he isn't dead. But no thanks to you, your brother is stuck in a wheelchair for the rest of his life. But he is alive? And strangely enough he didn't ask me to give you his warmest regards. You didn't answer my question. That was you wasn't it?'

'Yeah, that was me, and now you're here for revenge. So go on, shoot me, if you've got the balls to kill me in cold blood.'

'Oh believe me, I've thought about doing nothing else for seven long months. But I was persuaded not to murder you, because that would only reduce me to someone who is no better than you. Believe it or not, that was by Nathan himself. And his wife. So instead I've decided to give you a fair chance Jake. Just like it used to be in the days of The Old West. It's fitting for where we are now isn't it. In the heart of Texas. I can almost feel a song coming on. It's your choice Jake. Either I can arrest you and take you in, or, you can slowly pull out your gun and hold it down by your side. I'll hold mine in the same way, but I won't move until I see you start to raise yours. Then at least when I shoot you I'll have a clear conscience. And by the way, if you do manage to shoot me first, don't bother thinking about going looking for Cassidy, or his mother. He's dying of cancer and only got a few weeks to live at most, and she died a month ago.'

'Good,' Barclay growled, 'that's saved me the trouble of killing them after I've killed you then hasn't it.'

Lionel ignored the comment.

'How d'you find me?' he said.

'An extra-large peperoni pizza with all the trimmings. You used a debit card to pay for it. I hope that you enjoyed it, because that's what flagged up and alerted people to here, those people being the CIA. Also, you used your card to pay your cleaning company. They were very helpful too, they told me when your cleaner was next due. But you got me instead.'

Barclay said nothing, he just glared at Lionel. All the hatred which he'd kept under control during the previous months with Krystal bubbled to the surface and burned in his eyes.

'Anyway,' Lionel said, 'that doesn't matter now does it? Because I'm here. So, Jake, you choose. How do you want to play this out?'

Barclay stood stock still while he contemplated what to do.

Then, with his evil mind made up, he said, 'OK, El Lion, 'cos that's who you are ain't it? Let's go for it. It'll be my greatest pleasure to blow you away. Then I can get on with the rest of my life in peace.'

He slowly moved his right arm behind him and gripped the butt of his Glock. But instead of bringing it to his side he threw himself to the left and brought the pistol up, aiming it squarely at Lionel's centre mass and fired. But the bullet sailed harmlessly through thin air and shattered a gold framed floor to ceiling mirror which hung behind where Lionel had been standing. Barclay had missed because Lionel anticipated exactly what Barclay would do, and he was ready. He dived in the opposite direction and while in mid-air he shot Barclay between his eyes, killing him instantly. Barclay crumpled to the floor.

With no show of emotion Lionel stood up, went over and peered down at the body of his cousin. This time there could be no doubt. Jake Barclay was definitely dead. He turned and walked out of the house, leaving the front door ajar and got back into the van. He started the engine, turned the van around and drove slowly away from the ranch. Two miles down the road he pulled over into a secluded spot in the brush and parked behind a navy blue sedan. He got out of the van, walked around to the back of the sedan and opened the back. Laying bound on the floor, violently shaking with fear, gagged and blindfolded was Barclay's real agency cleaner. Lionel leaned over him.

'I'm sorry about that my friend,' he said removing the gag. 'What's your name?'

'After what you just done to me, trussing me up like a fucking Christmas turkey, you're calling me your friend?'

'I'm sorry, I really am, if you'll let me explain I'm sure you'll understand.' He gently pulled him upright, then pulled a knife from an open tool-box and cut the ropes, releasing the man's hands and feet, but he left the blindfold in place.

'It's what it says on the van,' the man rasped through a dry throat. 'Alf, but everyone calls me Uncle Alf.'

'Well, it's OK,' Lionel said, 'you can come out now Uncle Alf, he said, helping him out of the trunk. Listen, like I said, I'm sorry about that Alf, but I did promise you that no harm would come to you, and I've kept my word.'

He gave Alf a moment or two to regain his composure. 'Are you OK now?'

'Am I OK? OK? Are you fucking crazy man? What the hell was that all about? Are you so desperate to do a bit of cleaning you got to tie me up like a cow ready for branding and steal my van? What is it with you man? And I'll bet that you're a white dude! And why don't you take this fucking blindfold off me?'

'Not yet, we've got some business to do first.'

'Business, what business? I don't want to do no business with you. I've probably lost my job now, so why would I want to be even talking to you?'

'As I told you Alf, I mean Uncle Alf, I'm sorry. It was just something I had to do. It's done now, so take this and I'll be on my way.' He lifted Alf's right hand and placed a thick package into it.

'What's this?' Alf asked suspiciously.

'Twenty-five grand.'

Alf's voice rose by at least three octaves. 'Twenty-five grand, what the hell is that for?'

'It's for you to forget you ever saw me. It's for you to drive back to that ranch house and report a dead body, as if you only just got there. There's a cell phone in there with the cash as well. It's got one number programmed in it. Call it and ask to speak to Detective Les Curtis. He'll be expecting you to call and know what you're going to tell him. The door to the ranch is unlocked so you only have to say that you walked in when you got no answer and saw him lying there. Then get back in your van and drive away.'

'Dead body? What are you saying? That you just walked on into his house and killed the guy?'

'Yes, I did. Like I just told you. I had to.'

Alf thought for a moment. 'Well then, that depends,' he said.

'On what Alf?'

'On why you had to kill him.'

'He killed my wife, members of my family, plus some very good friends of mine and too many other people to list. Should I go on?'

'Shee-it, no need son. If that's true, and I don't know why I believe you, but I suppose I do, cos why in blazes would you say somethin' like that it if it wasn't. So I guess the bastard had it coming to him for a mighty long time. I never liked him anyway. He was a right miserable mother-finger!

'Mother-finger,' Lionel said. 'What's a mother-finger?'

'There's another word like it that the guys all use. But I won't say it. It's too disrespectful to my mother.'

'I'm sure there are plenty of others you could use. A lot better than mother-finger.'

'What are you? A fucking English teacher now as well as a killer?'

'No, I'm just saying that there's other.....'

'OK.' Alf interrupted. 'Son of a bitch then, is that better?'

'That will do nicely Alf, Lionel said.'

'Listen, this conversation is all very nice and all

but we ain't in no partnership here. You ain't no Bob Hope and I ain't no Sammy Davis. For a start, from what I can tell you ain't American and I definitely ain't Jewish!'

'Bob Hope was born in England Alf.'

'Really, are you shitting me?'

'No Alf, I promise you I'm not kidding. He was born in South London actually.'

Lionel was enjoying the relief of the banter with Alf. He felt the tension of the last months draining away. Then the realisation of why they were both there in the first place came back and slammed him in the gut like a sledgehammer. Like the punches he landed on Ruby and Canon all those years ago in the boxing ring at Edgeworth school, when his story began. Rebecca, his wife, murdered. Jake Barclay, dead, killed by him in retribution. The clock was ticking, he needed to get things back on track.

'Look Alf, take the money, go back to the ranch, make the phone call. Destroy the sim card, throw the phone away and then go home and enjoy the rest of your life.'

'You don't need to pay me nothin' son. I won't

say nothing. I sure as hell don't want you ever coming back here looking for me.'

Lionel said, 'don't worry Alf, I won't be coming back for you. Buy yourself something nice. You've earned it. I put you through a lot to get this done. Just one thing though.'

'What's that?'

'Turn around and don't take the blindfold off till you hear me drive away. It'll only be a few minutes. I've got to make some calls from the car first. Then I'll be leaving.'

Alf thought for a second or two. 'Well, I guess for twenty-five grand I can give you a few minutes. And we could use the money, a new car maybe. This here van belongs to the leasing company, and my old jalopy is about to pack up and die. And my wife's been moaning at me to do up the house a bit. It could do with a lick of paint here and there. The porch needs repairing too. Yes sir, you got yourself deal.' He transferred the package to his left hand, and held out his right.

'Thanks, and stay safe Mister Englishman,' he said.

They shook hands. 'I will Uncle Alf, I will, and

thank you.'

Alf turned around and listened, waiting for the sound of the car engine to start up. He heard the crunching of the man's footsteps as he walked slowly away and breathed a sigh of relief when he realised that he hadn't been shot in the back.

Lionel walked purposefully towards his car, hurled the Beretta deep into the brush, opened the door and almost collapsed into the driver's seat.

He pulled out a burn phone and keyed in a number.

The call was answered on the first ring.

'Hello.'

'Nathan, its Lionel. It's done, Barclay is dead. And it went down as you wanted, I gave him an opportunity to turn himself in, but he didn't take it. It was in self-defence, he went for his gun first. I'll phone Curtis and tell him to expect a call to tell him where to find the body. I've a few quick calls to make then I'll be on my way back. The flight from Fort Worth is in an hour. I should be with you by three in the morning.'

'Thanks Lionel, I don't know what else to say,

other than thanks, oh, and Abbey sends her love.'

Lionel ended the call, and punched in another number.

The recipient answered on the first ring.

'Curtis.'

'Hey Les, its Lionel. I'm in Texas.'

'Texas! What the hell are you doing there? You told me you were going back to England.'

'Listen up Les. Any moment now you're going to get a telephone call to your cell from a guy called Alf. He's going to report a dead body.'

'How'd you know this? What body? And how did he get my cell number?'

'I know it because I killed the guy whose body he's going to find. I told him where to find it and I gave him your number. I told him to call you.'

'You're not making any sense Lion. What body? Who did you kill?'

Lionel paused and the silence that hung on the line over the nine hundred and fifty odd miles between Chicago and Dallas was almost palpable.

'It's Jake Barclay Les. I just killed Jake Barclay. I

located him and I shot him.'

'Fuck. Lionel. How did you find him? One minute, it was that strange guy who called the office a week or so back wasn't it? He told you and you went off on your own didn't you? And you lied to me. You told me you were going home. Lionel, are you nuts? You could've been killed. You should have let us go in, or at least go with you. You're not some fucking vigilante!'

'I had to Les. It was the only way I could live with myself. You have to understand that. Anyway, if you'd have gone in mob-handed he'd have seen you and there would have been another bloody massacre. Just like outside O'Halloran's. So I went in to his house posing as his cleaner. Then I told him who I was and I offered him a chance to come in. He didn't take it. He went for his gun, first, so I shot him. It was self- defence Les, all very legal and kosher, I swear it. But it's over now. Barclay is dead, he won't be murdering anybody else, and your team can come and pick up his body. Listen, Les, I've got to get going. Keep your line clear. The guy is called Alf and he'll be calling you in about fifteen minutes. He's got nothing to do with it other than I told him where the body is and I persuaded him to call and tell you. But I gave him a bit of a hard time, so go easy on him, please.'

'OK,' Les sighed resignedly. When will you be back?'

'I won't be coming back Les. I've done what I stayed on here for. Say goodbye to the guys for me. It's been a privilege working with you all. If you look in the bottom right hand of my desk drawer you'll find my badge, and a letter of resignation. I left it all there in case, well hoping really, that things went this way. I'm going back to Washington now, then home to my family. And thanks for letting me stay at your lace too.'

Les detected the finality in Lionel's tone, but he also sensed that it was tinged with some sadness, because Lionel was talking about going home to a family which didn't include Rebecca.

'No Lion, the privilege has been ours. Stay safe my friend, and keep in touch.'

Lionel ended the call, and immediately made another. A woman answered the phone, which surprised Lionel.

'Hi, I'm sorry to call so late, but I was hoping to

speak to Lance Cassidy.'

'Who's calling?'

'I'm a friend of his. I'm calling to give him some information which he asked for.'

'Well this is Anne, his sister,' the woman said quietly. In a sad voice she added, 'I'm afraid that Lance passed away this afternoon.'

'Oh,' Lionel said. 'I'm very sorry to hear that. Lance was a good man. Please convey my condolences to the family.'

Lionel broke the connection. He looked through the numbers he had pre-programmed into the phone. Finding the one he wanted he pressed the button. It took a few seconds to connect, then on the second ring Nigel Fletcher answered in a sleepy voice.

'Hello, who is this?'

'Sir, it's Streat.'

Immediately awake and ignoring the fact that he'd been disturbed at 4.30 in the morning Fletcher said, 'Streat, what news do you have for me?'

'It's done sir. Barclay is dead.'

'Will there be any repercussions?'

'None at all sir?'

'Good. Well get yourself home Streat. I want you to head up the Prime Minister's protection detail. There are some major issues here. Oh, I do like what I just did there, major issues.' Fletcher laughed and hung up the phone before Lionel had a chance to answer.

Baffled, Lionel thought for a moment, then the penny dropped. Even at 4.30, having just been woken up, Fletcher's brain was whip fast. Fletcher was using a play on words. The Prime Minister was John Major.

Welcoming the relief and unable to resist a chuckle himself, Lionel stepped from the car, took the sim card out of the disposable cell phone, snapped it in half and tossed it away. Then he dropped the phone on to the road and crushed it under his heel. He got back into the car.

Then he took a tape recorder out of his inside pocket. His insurance, his proof, should he ever need it, that he had killed Barclay in self-defence. He rewound rewind the tape and waited anxiously for a moment or two. Then he pressed "play".

A tinny sounding recording started to play, but

the voices were unmistakeable. His and Barclay's. Good, the machine hadn't broken when he had dived to the floor to avoid Barclay's bullet.

Lionel: *That was you wasn't it?'*

Barclay: *'Yeah, that was me, and now you're here for revenge. So go on, shoot me, if you've got the balls to kill me in cold blood.'*

'Oh believe me, I've thought about doing nothing else for seven long months. But I was persuaded not to murder you, because that would only reduce me to someone who is no better than you. Believe it or not, that was by Nathan himself. And his wife. So instead I've decided to give you a fair chance Jake. Just like it used to be in the days of The Old West. It's fitting for where we are now isn't it. In the heart of Texas. I can almost feel a song coming on. It's your choice Jake. Either I can arrest you and take you in, or, you can slowly pull out your gun and hold it down by your side. I'll hold mine in the same way, but I won't move until I see you start to raise yours. Then at least when I shoot you I'll have a clear conscience. And by the way, if you do manage to shoot me first,

don't bother thinking about going looking for Cassidy, or his mother. He's dying of cancer and only got a few weeks to live at most, and she died a month ago.'

'Good, that's saved me the trouble of killing them after I've killed you then hasn't it. How d'you find me?'

'An extra-large peperoni pizza with all the trimmings. You used a debit card to pay for it. I hope that you enjoyed it, because that's what flagged up and alerted people to here, those people being the CIA. Also, you used your card to pay your cleaning company. They were very helpful too, they told me when your cleaner was next due. But you got me instead.'

'Anyway, that doesn't matter now does it? Because I'm here. So, Jake, you choose. How do you want to play this out?'

'OK, El Lion, 'cos that's who you are ain't it? Let's go for it. It'll be my greatest pleasure to blow you away. Then I can get on with the rest of my life in peace.'

Seconds later, two shots were heard on the tape, within a second of each other, but in that second there was the noise of glass shattering, proving beyond doubt that Barclay had fired first.

Lionel looked at his reflection in the driver's mirror and thought that he could detect the relief on his face.

'Let's go home,' he said to himself.

He started the car and drove away, leaving Alf still standing at the side of the road, waiting for the sound of the engine to fade into the distance. As soon as he could no longer hear it he removed the blindfold, and stared down in disbelief at the bundle of cash he was clutching in his clammy hand. He looked up to the heavens and laughed out loud at his good fortune. He jumped back into the van, stashed the cash under the seat and drove back to the ranch to see out his part of the deal.

In the suburbs of Washington, Nathan Weiss eased the lever on his electric wheelchair forward to move it over to the fireplace. He stopped in front of it and tossed his disposable cell phone into the flames, where it all crackled and spat loudly as it burned and melted over the smoking white hot logs.

And so, Barclay, his murderous brute of a brother who he had never shared an affectionate moment with, was finally dead. This time there could be no doubt. The long saga was finally over. He let out a weary sigh, not sure if it was from relief or in sadness. He turned his wheelchair around and went to the bedrooms at the other end of his new purpose-built bungalow. He steered it into his son's bedroom to check on him. His month old son was sleeping soundly. The boy was named Peleh, which means miracle, and was a reference to the awful night when the second baby, who had shared his and Peleh's mother's womb, was killed, but he had miraculously survived. Nathan sat with Peleh in the approaching darkness for a few moments. He brought his hand up to his mouth and kissed it, then he laid it gently onto Peleh's forehead, being careful not to disturb the child. Then he went out and across to his own bedroom. He manoeuvred the wheelchair over to the bed. Without bothering to undress reached for the handle of the pulley, which was hanging from the ceiling, hauled himself onto the bed and laid down, cuddling Abbey closely until he fell into a peaceful sleep.

Alf pulled up in his van at Barclay's ranch. He slowly opened the driver's door and stepped down onto the gravel and nervously stepped towards the front door. A bright red brand Mercedes convertible was parked right outside. He could hear the "tick-tick" from the engine as it cooled down. He tried to lighten his footsteps as they crunched on the gravel and flapped his hands at it willing it to hush up. The front door was wide open. He wondered if it had been left like that by his recent benefactor.

As he gingerly got closer to the house he could hear someone crying bitterly. He peered through into the wide hallway and he could see a beautiful woman kneeling over the bloodied corpse of the ranch owner. His legs were bent at odd angles beneath his huge body. She sobbed as tears streamed down her flaming cheeks.

'Don't you worry Jake' she wailed. 'I'll find who did this to you and rip his face off. I'll make him suffer. I promise you that honey.'

Then she looked up and saw Alf standing there.

'What the fuck are you doing here Alf?'

'It's my day for cleaning Miss Krystal. I'm sorry

I'm late.'

'Well you ain't needed now. Go home, just go home.'

Then Krystal Brown turned her attention back to the lifeless body of Jake Barclay. She held his face close to hers, whispering into his now deaf ear, vowing to get her revenge, and already imagining the awful lengths that she would go to in order to exact it. Then, as self-preservation kicked in she suddenly realised.

"I can't be here. It won't take the cops long to work out that this is Jake. And I can't be associated with him, not with all the shit he's done. And if they find me here they might look into Aristos's mugging again. They'll soon realise that was Jake as well and that will be me totally fucked. I have to get away from here now, fast."

She picked up her bag and rushed outside and caught up with Alf who was scurrying back to his van. She grabbed hold of him by the shoulder and whirled him around.

'I was never here Alf, you never saw me, got it?'

'Yes ma'am, I mean no ma'am'.

She dipped her hand into her bag and pulled

out a wad of cash. This is for your trouble, and your silence,' she said. 'But if you blab, I'll hunt you down, and when I find you I promise you it won't be a pleasant experience for you.' She grabbed his hand and pressed the cash into it. Then she strode to her Mercedes, got in and roared in a flurry of gravel, leaving Alf standing there shaking with fear.

He got into his van and looked in his hand at the bundle of cash. They were all one hundred dollar bills.

"Fuck me, there must be at least three grand there," he thought. Regaining control of himself he marvelled at what had happened to him over the last hour or so.

"What a fucking day this had turned out to be. Two people have given me more cash than I've seen in years. Just to keep a secret. Well, I can certainly manage that. You bet your dammed life I can."

He drove out of the ranch and parked on the roadside. He fished the cell phone out of the package which Lionel had given him. He found the pre-programed number and pressed the button to call it. When the call was answered he said, 'My name is Alf, I want to report a dead body.' Then as instructed by Lionel he gave the address, disconnected the call, took out the sim-card, broke it between his fingers and tossed the phone out of the van window and into the brush. Then, grinning widely from ear to ear he drove home.

THE END

ACKNOWLEDGEMENTS

First, as always, Roo, who as with my first two books patiently put up with me while I tried to ignore most of what else was going on around us while I was concentrating on writing this, my third.

To the many people who read "Kill or Cure" and observed that I had left the story ready for the sequel. Well, here it is, I hope you enjoy it, and think that it fits in well with "El Lion, A Life Not Lived", which I had to get out of my system first.

To our dearest friends, The Bushey Legends, who never complained about my one-track conversation, which was focussed on how many words or pages I was up to, even though I am sure they must have tired of hearing it. Being the good friends that that are they never complained, well, not to me anyway.

To my editors, Roo, Jackie, Pedro and Rocki for their scrupulous checking and valued advice.

And of course, to my fabulous family, those ever-sustaining lights of my life, who are always there for me with their wonderful warmth, lavish love and endless encouragement.

Look out for the next book in the series
KRYSTAL CLEAR
Coming Soon!